*Q*uinton was mesmerized by the delightful sound
of her laughter. He wished he could think of a
reason to draw his visit out longer. Instead, he
did the gentlemanly thing and headed for the
front door with her following close behind him. He
stopped at the door and turned and stared at Angela, who
was a captivating vision with her eyes a bit drowsy and
her hair mussed. His heart raced and his mouth grew
dry from the erotic thoughts that went straight from his
mind to his maleness. He swallowed hard. "Good night,
Angela," he said in a quiet tone. He leaned down and
placed a brief, gentle kiss on her forehead. Touching his
lips to the warm flesh of her forehead, he closed his eyes
to relish the jolt of tenderness he experienced. He struggled with himself to keep from enfolding her in his arms
and crushing her to him. He was flooded with emotion
when she reached up and hugged him the way a grateful
friend would. She murmured her thanks once again and
released him.

Enjoy these titles

by
Sinclair LeBeau

So Amazing

Glory of Love

Somebody's Someone

Your Precious Love

by

Sinclair LeBeau

Indigo Love Stories
Sensuous

Genesis Press, Inc.
315 Third Avenue North
Columbus, MS 39701

This book may not be reproduced in whole or in part, by mimeograph or any other means, without permission. Published in the United States of America by The Genesis Press, Inc. For information write The Genesis Press, Inc., 315 3rd Avenue North, Columbus, MS 39701.

Copyright© 2001 by Linda Smith

Your Precious Love

First Edition

Chapter 1

Riley, Virginia

The forbidding gray October sky burst with rain the moment that Angela Etheridge zoomed into a parking space at the Sedgewick Mall. Without giving a thought to getting drenched or chilled by the crispness of the fall day, she hopped out of her car, forgetting her coat and dashing through the mall's main entrance. She marched down the hall that led to the security office as if she were on a mission. Her mind had been so muddled by anxiety and fear that she was unaware of the tall man easing up behind her. Lost in her thoughts, she made her way toward her destination. Suddenly, the man hooked his hand around her right arm and pulled her toward him.

Sinclair LeBeau

Angela gasped and her heart stood still. Frightened to her core, she whirled around to gaze into the face of a man who wore sunshades and a baseball cap. When she scowled, the man chuckled and removed his sunshades, shoving them into the pocket of his jacket. Her fearful expression melted into one of relief when she recognized Quinton Gibbs, best friend of her late husband, Cole. She gave the man a querulous smile and pulled away from him, frowning. "My goodness, Quinton. You nearly gave me a heart attack." She placed a trembling hand over her racing heart. Seeing him filled her with a mixture of emotions that she didn't want to deal with, especially now.

A couple of teen boys passed them and ogled Quinton. They chorused, " 'Sweet Que, the Man.' "

Quinton acknowledged the boys with a smile and a jerk of his head as if to say, "What's up?"

Then he returned his attention to Angela with a look of concern. "Believe me, my intentions weren't to frighten you. I merely wanted to say hello. I haven't seen you or that son of yours since...since the...uh, Cole's funeral two years ago." His eyes darkened with pain.

At the mention of her husband's funeral, Angela grew somber and even more anxious to get away from him. "I'm in a hurry, Quinton. I don't have time to socialize," she said in a brusque tone. She turned away and hustled toward her destination. He was beginning to draw curious onlookers. She figured the two boys must have spread the word that the pro athlete was in the mall. She didn't want to be bothered by the attention that Quinton would draw. More important, she wanted to keep her reason for coming to the mall private.

Watching her flee, Quinton was troubled by the panicked look he had observed in her eyes. She was unusually agitated and his gut feeling told him it had nothing to do with her dislike for him. He understood why she had shut him out of her and her son's life and he had respected her wish for him to stay away. Yet, he had always felt responsible for her and to that boy of hers. Cole, his beloved deceased friend, would have wanted him to be around for them.

With this thought in mind, Quinton took off after Angela even though he knew she would resent his intrusion. But it was time for them to forget all that stuff that had happened in the past and hopefully to resume the friendship they'd once shared. After all, there was a child to consider. Quinton had often thought about the boy and wondered how he was making out with his father no longer around to guide him. There was no doubt in Quinton's mind that Cole would want him to be there for his son. Only Quinton's obligations to his pro basketball career had kept him from resolving his differences with Angela in order to stay close to Tyson. But now that he had been forced into retirement because he had ruined his knee, he wanted to make up for lost time with Angela and, most importantly, with Cole's son,

Tyson. Since his basketball career was over, he had returned to live in Riley, Virginia, and operate several businesses. Ever since his return, Angela and Tyson had been on his mind. He had been trying to figure out a way to approach her without antagonizing her. Today, fate had given him an opportunity to set things right. Seeing her worried expression, he was determined that he wasn't going to let Angela keep Tyson away from him anymore. The boy needed a man in his life. Angela was going to have to respect his feelings and remember that he had loved Cole like a brother, he mused. She was going to have to respect the fact that he had suffered a loss just as much as she and Tyson had. He missed the man who had grown up with him and had been his friend long before he had gained celebrity on the NBA basketball courts. Cole had seen him at his best and at his worst and still managed to love him. Cole's friendship had always been a source of comfort, especially when the glamour and the pitfalls of being a superstar athlete got to be more than he ever dreamed it would be.

With determined strides, Quinton's six-foot-four inch frame allowed him to catch up to Angela's hurried pace. "I want to know about Tyson. I think about him all the time and I would love to come by and see him," he said in a no nonsense tone. Seeing how her brow crumpled with impatience, he grew annoyed. When in the world was this woman going to let bygones be bygones? he thought. "I want to get reacquainted with him. Kids will forget you once you're out of their lives. Cole would have wanted it that way and you know it."

Quinton's interest and demand to see Tyson rattled Angela's nerves. She didn't want to go into this with him, not today of all days. Staring up at Quinton, she held her lips tightly together and swallowed, holding back her emotions. Her eyes glistened suddenly with tears that spilled over from the corners. She glanced away from him to gather herself, but her facade broke. She began to openly sob.

Seeing her emotional display unnerved Quinton. It was the last thing he expected from the petite woman who had been so proud and defiant when he had caught up to her. Her misery tore at his heart. He placed a caring hand on her arm. "What's the matter? What's going on, Angela?" he asked. His deep voice was full of concern. "Talk to me. I'm not leaving until you let me know what's going on." He reached inside his jacket and pulled out a handkerchief and handed it to her.

She accepted it and wiped her eyes. His kindness made her feel ashamed for being rude to him. Despite her issues with him, she was touched by his persistent interest and concern. She had forgotten that one of his better qualities had been his willingness to listen and to always come up with some kind of solution. Being on her own with a teen son wasn't easy. She had no idea what to do with the sweet little boy who had become this manchild who was determined to do things his way, usually ending up in some kind of mess. Since Tyson had turned thirteen a few months ago, she had been faced with issues and challenges that made her doubt her capabilities as a parent. She had kept her insecurities to herself for fear that anyone she shared them with would judge her and think that she was a bad mother. After all, she had chosen to go back to work and open her own bookstore, All of Our Best, when she really hadn't needed to financially. Angela wrapped her arms around her body, comforting herself. She lowered her head and her shoulders drooped with the shameful burden she had to bear today. "Uh...Tyson is in the security office, Quinton. He's being held there for shoplifting." Her voice quivered with emotion and tears of fear drizzled down her face.

Placing a caring hand on her shoulder, Quinton's face crinkled with concern. "Oh no! I'm sorry," he declared softly. "How can I help you?"

Gazing up at him, Angela was comforted by the sincerity she saw on his face. She was glad that he offered his support. However, she was reluctant to accept it. "It's kind of you to want to help, but I'll be okay. Once I see what's going on and get them to release him, I'll...we'll be just fine," she responded, trying to bolster her confidence. She offered him his handkerchief back, but he insisted she keep it. She pursed her lips with a weak smile and clutched the handkerchief to her chest "I really have to go and handle this," she said, turning and walking briskly away to fetch her son.

Just as Angela reached out to push open the door of the mall security office, Quinton's long form stepped in front of her. He gave her an encouraging smile. "I can't let you face this alone. I just know Cole wouldn't like it one bit."

Exhaling deeply, Angela gave him an appreciative look and allowed him to hold open the door for them to go rescue Tyson.

Angela approached the no-nonsense looking woman dressed in a uniform behind the desk. "I'm here for my son, Tyson Etheridge. I'm his mother."

The security guard stared at Angela briefly and then her attention fell on Quinton, who stood behind her. "Hey, you're Quinton Gibbs, that NBA player who retired last year," she enthused, ignoring Angela's request. "How's that busted knee?" The stocky woman grinned with interest.

"That's me. I'm okay, ma'am," he admitted quietly. "Listen, we've come concerning her son, Tyson Etheridge. Could you please help us?"

The security guard gave Angela an apologetic look and rose from her seat. "Sure thing. I'll let my supervisor know you're here." She disappeared from the reception area into a hallway in the suite of offices.

Anxiously waiting for the woman's return, Angela rocked back and forth on her heels. Worrying over what would become of Tyson for his senseless deed, she was hit by a wave of apprehension.

Noticing Angela's distress, Quinton leaned on the counter near her. "It's going to be all right," he assured her in a calm tone. "I'm here. I'll call one of my attorneys if it's necessary. At his age, I'm certain that it's fixable."

At the mention of attorneys, Angela's heart twisted with icy fear. Hopefully, there would be no need to haul her son to court. She nibbled on her bottom lip and closed her eyes, grunting at the mere thought of the judicial system. She prayed that these people weren't planning on involving the police.

The female security officer returned and announced, "You can come this way, Mrs. Etheridge."

Angela locked eyes with Quinton, who looked as though he was waiting for permission to accompany her. "It's best I see him alone. I'll be okay," she told Quinton, trying to convince herself. She heaved a sigh and followed the officer who led the way back down the hallway.

"I'll be here waiting," Quinton called after her.

Angela glanced over her shoulder at him and lavished a grateful look upon him.

Walking to the office where her son was being kept, Angela was relieved to see Tyson, though he sat slumped and angry at a long table with a middle-aged male officer.

The sight of her son being held weighed heavy on

her heart. She gave her son a chiding look and focused on the officer. "Can you tell me exactly what happened today? No one would give me any details over the phone."

Tyson shifted petulantly in his seat and folded his arms and buried his face there as though he wanted to shut out this moment.

Angela poked Tyson on the shoulder. "Sit up and listen," she insisted. She stared at the officer. "Could you tell me what happened?"

The officer spoke in a dry tone. "Ma'am, your son was caught stealing several CDs from the Wall of Music. According to the employees, this wasn't the first incident of this young man and his friends hitting their store. He just happened to get caught this time. We had a plain-sclothes officer staking the store and he nabbed him this time. His partners in crime got away."

Listening to the man, Angela tried to maintain her dignity though her face burned with shame. Feeling dismayed, she stared at her son. "I'm sorry for his behavior. It's so unlike him, officer. My son is a good child," she explained to the man who had a blank expression. "I'll be more than happy to pay for whatever has been taken from the store. And I'll guarantee you that he won't do anything like this again." Though her heart was bruised by her child's action, her stance was stiff and proud.

The man rubbed his hand across his gray and black

crew-cut hair and gave her a dubious look. "I certainly hope that it doesn't happen again. Well, he won't have the opportunity to do it any time soon. Under the circumstances, we're going to have to ban him from that store for the next six months. If he's caught in there, then we might be forced to call in the police," he informed her, giving Tyson an admonishing look. "And I'd like to remind you that he won't be allowed in this mall unless he's with an adult. That's our policy for first time juvenile shoplifters who are caught."

Instead of looking at the officer, Tyson fidgeted with the fancy watch that his mother had given him for his birthday a few months ago.

Angela shook Tyson on the shoulder to get his attention. "Did you hear that, Tyson? Do you understand the seriousness of all this?" Her voice was firm. Tyson shifted restlessly in his seat. "Yeah, yeah, I heard him," he said, sulking.

Stress lines formed on her brow. "You'll have no more problems from him," she said, praying in heart that this would be so. "Can we please go now?"

The officer shoved a clipboard with some papers on it toward her. "I need you to sign this, ma'am. It's a statement agreeing to what I've explained to you."

Angela picked up the clipboard and read the statement before scribbling her name on the bottom of the form. She handed it back to the man and touched Tyson on the shoulder to urge him to move. "Let's go," she ordered.

Without looking at her, Tyson bolted out his seat and stormed out of the room, leaving his mother to trail behind him.

By the time she returned to the reception area, she found Tyson being held captive by Quinton. The dynamic looking man had placed his hands on the boy's shoulders and was assessing the teen. "Look at you, man. I can't believe how much you've grown. You're the spitting image of your old man. It's good to see you, man." Despite the awkward circumstances of their meeting, Quinton beamed at the boy to show how glad he was to see him.

After a flash of admiration, Tyson stared uneasily. "Uncle Quinton, what are you doing back in Riley? I heard you had to retire from the NBA, but I thought this town would be the last place you'd want to hang around." He grinned. "If I was paid like you are, this town wouldn't ever see me again."

Quinton smiled at Tyson, recognizing the same restless and rebellious feelings he once had. "Man, this is my home. I'm living here now. Well, one of my homes is here," he explained. "The older you get, you learn that there's no place like home. In Riley, I can relax and have a bit more privacy than I do anywhere else." Quinton turned down the warmth in his expression and looked at the boy eye to eye. "What are you doing in the security office? You've upset your mother terribly," he admonished. "Your old man would be disappointed and..."

Tyson's brown eyes took on an angry glare. He frowned and turned his back to Quinton to face his mother who had been listening to their exchange. She took Tyson's hand in a comforting manner. But Tyson snatched it away and rushed out of the office into the hallway where a small group of onlookers stood peeking into the glass door of the security office, staring at "Sweet Que" Gibbs.

Angela could have done without the attention that Quinton had drawn. She was sure that word would get out that her child had been caught shoplifting. And it would be all because of the attention that Quinton brought to the situation. She stared at the group who were obviously die-hard fans of Quinton and then she stared at him. "We have to go and you have your fans to look after."

Quinton gave her a helpless look and turned away from the group outside the door. "I had no business speaking to Tyson that way. I've become a stranger to him; I was out of place coming on so strong."

Angela ran her hand through her raven hair as though wiping away her worries. "Yes, you were. He's been through enough without you of all people reminding him of how he has not lived up to his father's expectations." Suddenly she was anxious to be away from Quinton. She regretted letting down her guard and allowing him into her life, her problems. "I appreciate your interest," she said in a controlled voice. "It's...it's been good seeing you, but I have to get Tyson home. Everything will be just fine. I'm going to restrict him to the house until he's eighteen." She chuckled nervously at her silly reasoning to make Quinton think that she was in control now that the crisis had passed. She hated the dubious look Quinton gave her. It made her feel insecure and gave her all the more reason to escape from him.

Standing tall with his arms folded at his waist, Quinton looked regal, she mused. She noticed how he twisted his mouth thoughtfully, as though choosing his words before verbalizing them. As she went for the door Quinton spoke.

Standing near her, Quinton said, "I can imagine it's not easy raising by yourself a growing guy like Tyson with his hormones. Looks to me as though he's going to need some manly muscle to keep him in check. I'm living here now, Angela. I have several business interests and then my father and sister are here," he explained, noticing her aloof attitude. "Anyway," he said, reaching inside his jacket and pulling out a business card which he pressed into her hand, "I want you to call me..."

Angela protested. "That's not really necessary. I..."

"Hold up, Angela. Listen to me, will you?" He placed his hand on her arm, but she moved away from his touch. He continued, "You and I have had our issues in the past. But it's time to let that stuff go. Cole is gone." He cleared his throat as though it hurt to mention his

13

friend's name. "I'm concerned about Tyson. His welfare and future are more important than whatever happened in the past. You know as well as I do that Cole wouldn't want his kid in this kind of trouble. I might not know much about raising kids, but I'm willing to give it a shot for Tyson's sake." He stared at her in a manner that conveyed his sincerity. "Think about things for a couple of days. Give me a call so we can talk. I would hate for us...uh, you, to lose that kid to the streets. At his age, they're extremely seductive to young Black males," he warned.

She clutched his business card and crammed it into the pocket of her slacks, along with the handkerchief he had given her earlier to dry her tears. She gave Quinton a bland look to hide the feelings of shame she experienced for son's behavior. "Don't concern yourself over us. We're just going through a rough time like any family with a teen does," she said. "Bye, Quinton." She breezed out of the security office and through the small knot of gawkers that had gathered to get a look at "Sweet Que, the Man."

Reaching her son who waited in the hallway, she linked her arm into his and urged him to hurry along with her. Angela glanced back to see Quinton exiting the office and being surrounded by autograph seekers, who thrust bits of paper at him. Quinton flashed a dazzling smile and chatted with the group while he signed an autograph for each of them. The female security officer stood near him as though she had been hired to protect him.

Quinton must have felt Angela staring, because he glanced up and caught her looking. He winked at her and stared wistfully.

Angela quickly shifted her glance and hustled her petulant son out of the mall.

Once she and Tyson had returned to her car and headed for home in the bumper to bumper traffic of the rainy evening, Angela hoped that Tyson's mall incident had scared him enough not to repeat the action again. She wanted this to be the last time that she would have to get her son out of trouble. She thought of the judgmental look on Quinton's face and regretted how she had broken down in front of him. He was the last person that she wanted to appear helpless around. Sitting at a stoplight in the congested traffic, she dug in the pocket of her slacks and retrieved the handkerchief and the business card. She turned on the little light on the dashboard so that she could read the card. Quinton's Corner–Sports Bar was printed in bold gold letters. On the card were also various phone numbers, a pager number, and the address of his business. She sighed thoughtfully. What in the world could that hot shot superstar athlete, philanderer, and liar teach her son? What kind of mentor would he make? She bitterly remembered the betrayer Quinton had been a few years ago. She considered ripping the card and tossing it out the window and into the wet streets. Then she glanced over her shoulder at her sullen son slumped in the back seat who had no male figures in his life to relate to now that his father was deceased. She considered the blank, angry look that her son walked around with most of the time, along with his I-don't-care-attitude. A cold chill of fear went through her when she thought of what Quinton had said about how seductive the streets could be to an impressionable young black male. She took Quinton's business card and handkerchief and tucked them carefully back into the pocket of her slacks. Waiting in the slow traffic, she rubbed her face pensively with her forefinger and thumb. Quinton's cologne clung to her flesh from her handling his handkerchief. It was a nice fragrance, Angela thought, reconsidering Quinton's offer to mentor Tyson.

Chapter 2

Later that day after Quinton had seen Angela, he entered the house of his sister, Jessica Frazier, through the back door that led into her kitchen, carrying an oversized box. He found his father Calvin alone amidst the kitchen clutter and the abundance of food that had been prepared for the fifth birthday party of his niece Stacey.

Greeting his son with a smile, Calvin Gibbs sipped from a can of beer while watching a game on the portable television. "I thought you had ditched this confusion."

Under his father's curious stare, Quinton carefully placed the gift-wrapped box that was for his niece on the floor. He knew his father wanted to know what he had purchased, but to tease him he didn't volunteer any information. "There's no way I couldn't have come. The last person I need to have angry with me is Jessica. You know how she is about us being together for these family occasions."

His father, a brawny man, nodded and eyed the big box, trying to guess what it could be. "You're trying to outshine everyone else's gift, huh? You show-off. Once little Stacey sees that big box she is going to forget about everyone else's gift." He shook his head, grinning. "Want a beer, son? I bought a twelve pack along for you and me. It's hidden in the pantry. I knew we'd need something more than punch and cake to get us through another evening of your sister bossing us around." He finished off his beer and tossed the can in the trash and then went to the pantry for another grocery store-chilled brew and tossed one to his son. "We can't let anyone see us drinking. Orders from your sister. She wants us to act as though we're saints for the day." He chuckled. The man's pecan-complexioned face glowed with affection for his caring and loving daughter who had assumed the role of family caregiver ever since his wife had run out on them.

Quinton laughed and popped the top on his beer and took a long drink. He savored the beer in his mouth before swallowing and speaking. "How's the party going?"

Without taking his focus from the television, Quinton's father said, "There's confusion and plenty of noise. The kids are having the time of their lives though, making a big mess that we're going to have to help clean up. I can take being out there in the trenches only a few minutes at a time. My nerves ain't what they used to be. That's why I'm hiding out here, fortifying myself." He glanced at his son. "We won't be safe long. Jessica plans to bring Stacey's birthday cake out and light the candles in a few minutes. She's running her poor husband Jeff every which a way. Poor man."

Quinton stood near his father to watch the extraordinary play of the college football game on television. "She's got him on the video camera, right? She had made that assignment to me, but I got out of it by calling and saying I would be late. I got held up at the mall by an old friend," he said, thinking of Angela. "Jessica was disappointed. She ordered me to get here as soon as I could. She reminded me in that no nonsense voice of hers that she wants all of us on video and in the pictures she's taking of the party today."

Quinton stared at the television though he had lost interest in the game. He couldn't get Angela Etheridge and her problem with Tyson out of his mind. He remembered when he first caught a glimpse of the woman in the mall. He'd had no idea that it was Angela. He had considered the sight of the shapely, attractive woman as eye candy. A delectable sight in tailored slacks and a pullover sweater that accentuated the best of her feminine qualities. Studying the young woman more closely, he had realized that it was Angela. The last time he had seen her she was wearing her hair really long and pulled back into a pony-tail. Angela usually dressed in sweat pants and shirts or either baggy jeans and t-shirts and she had been much heavier a few years ago. In other words, she had been a no-frills woman as most young housewives and stay-at-home moms were. The change that Angela had made was remarkable. Shorter hair and stylish clothes had turned her into quite a looker, he decided. Watching her, he was hit by a wave of nostalgia. He remembered how at one time he had been a welcomed friend in her home. It had taken everything in him to keep from calling out her name. Remembering the bad feelings between them, he felt that she would ignore him. Still, he had taken off behind her. Catching up to her and getting a closer look, he was amazed by how marvelous she looked. There was a girl-next-door look that was impressive. When he stopped to talk with her, he hadn't expected to get caught up in the trouble she was having with her son. Learning that little Tyson had been shoplifting was devastating to her, Quinton mused. Relating the incident to Quinton there in the mall had humiliated the proud woman. He hadn't been able to get the sight of the pain in her eyes or the sound of her heart-wrenching sobs out his mind. Tagging along with her to the security office, Quinton couldn't believe how big Tyson had grown. And he was outdone that the boy had chosen to dress to imitate those popular gangster rappers that appeared on the music videos. The anger that Tyson exhibited when Quinton mentioned his father had disturbed him as well. He wondered what could have caused the bright, endearing little fellow he remembered to want to be the way he was. Had it been the fact that his mother had allowed him to do as he pleased in his father's absence?

Calvin Gibbs poked his son on the arm. "Quinton, son, what's on your mind?"

Looking troubled, Quinton used his forefinger and his thumb to brush his mustache. "I ran into Angela, Angela Etheridge, in the mall," he said in a matter-of-fact tone.

Quinton's father walked to the other side of the kitchen and grabbed a couple of the mini-hot dogs on buns that had been left on a platter. Before popping one in his mouth, he said, "Oh boy! Did she talk to you? Is she still holding that grudge against you over Cole?"

"Unfortunately, she still has some bad feelings," Quinton said in a reflective tone. "But you should see Cole's boy, Tyson. Boy, has he grown. He's thirteen and could easily pass for a guy sixteen-years-old. I don't know what she's been feeding him, but he's shooting up fast."

His father now held the platter of hot dogs and ate yet another one. He gulped it down while studying his son's expression as he spoke of Angela and Tyson. "I'm surprised you got close to her. She has been awfully pissed with you. What did you two find to talk about?"

21

He smiled wryly.

Quinton rubbed the back of his neck and thought of the vulnerability Angela had let slip during her crisis. He hadn't been able to get it out of his mind. "Nothing much, Pop. She and I were talking one minute and the next thing I knew she was crying her heart out. Tyson had been caught shoplifting and was being held by security in the mall."

Shaking his head, showing his disappointment, Calvin exclaimed, "Dog gone it! What in the world has gotten into that boy? He deserves a good paddling. The kind that I know his mother can't lay on him."

Quinton twisted his mouth thoughtfully and said, "You know kids can't be disciplined that way anymore. They turn their parents in for stuff like that. Kids can cry child abuse. These kids have the law on their side these days."

"Humph," Calvin grunted. "Ain't no child abuse. When I was a boy, you could get your bottom warmed for looking the wrong way at your parents. It was what was done out of love to keep children in line. Parents handled their kids instead of letting outsiders deal with something that should be kept in the family. These fast kids are running their parents now. What are folks going to do with kids who seem to be going buck wild?" He shook his head. "Take you and your sister. I never had to spank you kids but once or twice. You knew I didn't have time to tolerate a lot of foolishness. When your mother left us to *find* herself, I couldn't afford to let either one of you run me. I knew people were watching me and waiting for me to mess up with you guys. You were only nine-years-old and your sister eleven. I had to prove to people that I could keep it together despite what your mother did. I had to be father and mother to you. And I did a damn good job, if I say so myself." He beamed at his son. "Both of you graduated from college. Your sister teaches high school English and married a good man, a military officer. And you had the sense to get a business degree despite the fact that those pro basketball agents were nibbling at you to draft you. I wouldn't have it. I didn't want you to get caught out here without any skills to fall back on once your playing time was up. You had a fabulous fishbowl career in the pros until you blew that knee of yours out. Just think. If I hadn't insisted you finish college, you wouldn't have had the business sense you have to invest your money the way you have."

Quinton gave his father a slow grin. "Dad, take it easy. I didn't mean to set you off, man. I was telling you about Angela and her problems. I'm concerned about her. She's stressed, Dad. She has too much pride to ask for help, but I know she needs it." His handsome face clouded with concern. " I don't know how she is going to manage Tyson all on her own." As he rubbed the side of his face thoughtfully, he caught his father looking at him. "What?"

"You shouldn't want to get involved with her. Look at how she lashed out at you about that Cole mess." He finished off his beer. "You're a better man than me. I would let her be. She made it clear to you after Cole died that she didn't want you around. Remember what a hassle it was for you to get her to let you be a pallbearer at Cole's funeral?"

Quinton cringed at the painful memory of that particular incident. "Man, was I glad that Cole's mother and aunt intervened and convinced Angela to let me do that. I would have been crushed had I not been able to be a part of the services to the guy who was like a brother to me."

His honey-colored eyes dimmed as he was hit anew by the grief that he thought he had let go of long ago. He had often wished that Angela hadn't shut him out of her life. They could have been such a comfort to each other. Both of them had loved Cole. During the early years of Cole and Angela's marriage, Quinton had been a bit envious that Angela had taken his running partner away from him. At the time, Quinton had believed she had gotten pregnant on purpose her freshman year in college. Cole had been a senior who had charmed the naive Angela Houston into a relationship that he had only considered one more conquest for himself and his reputation as a ladies' man on their college campus. Marriage wasn't what Cole had wanted. However, Angela had made it clear that she wasn't going to terminate her pregnancy.

She was a preacher's daughter and abortion went against her upbringing she had told Cole. Since Cole had never known his father, who had died of an aneurysm when he was a toddler, he felt obligated to Angela and to his unborn child to be around for him. He had loved his son the moment he first laid eyes upon him in the delivery room. But Cole never quite developed the kind of affection for Angela that a man is supposed to have for his wife. Unfortunately, Cole had slipped around with other women to escape the trap he felt his marriage had become. Though he was unhappy with Angela, he wouldn't leave her. He didn't want his son to grow up in a broken home. So, he had pretended that they were the happy family. Quinton remembered it all too clearly. Poor eager young Angela had done what she could to be a perfect wife, mother and homemaker. But Cole had shown no appreciation for her efforts.

"She blamed me for the problems they had in their marriage," Quinton told his father. "She got to the place where she resented the friendship Cole and I had. When I began to play pro ball, she considered me a bad influence. At the time, though, fast women and wild parties were part of my lifestyle. The temptation was sweet for someone like me who had come from a conservative town like Riley. Anyway, Angela made me feel as though I was a pimp to Cole. Believe me, I tried to keep Cole in line. Landing that job as a firefighter had given him new confidence in himself. He had worked in the mall, managing a men's clothing store until that time. He hated that job, but it paid the bills." Quinton grew pensive. "Cole had a mind of his own and a weakness for the pretty women that hung out at the places where my teammates and I used to hang to unwind. Though he wasn't an athlete, the women still gravitated to him, knowing he was a fireman. Women came on to him using all kinds of sexual innuendoes because of his job. They either wanted them to put out their fire or start some." Quinton grinned briefly with the memory.

"You weren't responsible for Cole acting like a knucklehead," Calvin said. "The man should have had sense enough to appreciate that woman. When you told me about his women on the side, I tried to talk to him. But you know how stubborn that Cole was. His mother and his aunt ruined him when they raised him. They were too strict with him. He wasn't allowed to hang out like the other fellows, he couldn't listen to certain music, he had to dress like they wanted him to. They didn't care what the styles were. They expected him to be a gentleman in every way. No one wanted to go around those sisters. Too many don'ts were involved. You've got to let kids be kids to a certain extent. If they can't have fun and relax at home, they'll go where they can. You can lose your kids being too firm. When he went to college, he got out of control and that Angela just got caught up in a relationship with him that she wasn't capable of dealing with. He messed with that girl's heart and her mind. It was a shame. She was a good girl. Then he had the audacity to act as though he was mad with the whole world because he had to get married and do what any man is supposed to do when they get a girl in trouble."

Quinton listened carefully to his father. Then he related more of the past. "Cole's weakness was always virginal girls. Most inexperienced girls like Angela are clueless about birth control. The first guy they sleep with is the one they trust and give their hearts to. Angela slept with Cole and fell head over heels in love with him. Since she had given him a special part of her, she expected him to want to be with her for always. Cole was used to getting what he wanted and walking away. But with Angela, he got much more than he bargained for. He ended up getting entangled in his game and losing all his dreams. He got Angela pregnant, got married when he had only a year left in college. Then when he got seasonal work in construction after he married, he dropped a cinder block on his foot and broke it so badly he couldn't play ball anymore. He lost his position on the basketball team and his desire to stay in college. He wanted to go pro with me. That had been our dream since we were kids."

"But all he could do was cling to that fantasy through you," Calvin said. "It was sad that he didn't have the sense to move on and to be grateful for what God gave him. A good woman and a healthy son." Calvin shook his head. "Then he makes his life a mess by letting his wife catch him with another woman in *your* house while you were with the team out of town. If I was her, I would have believed that you were in on all his carrying ons with other women too."

Quinton exhaled, remembering his frustration with his friend's behavior. "Oh man, I'll never forget that night Angela showed up checking on Cole. I don't know who tipped her off to this day. It must have been one of his other women that he had dogged out." He shook his head in disapproval of his friend's bad behavior. "I was dead tired. The team had just gotten in from the road after two exhausting games. Arriving from the air terminal and getting out of a taxi, I saw Cole's car and just figured he was hanging out at my place, watching a movie, drinking a few brews in my theater room. I called out for him when I hit the house. No answer. I thought the knucklehead had fallen asleep. I get to my bedroom and there he is, rolling in bed on my designer sheets with some honey. Man, oh man. I hit the roof. Then to add to all the confusion and anger, Angela shows up ready to kick butt. I tried to keep her from seeing him, but she pushed by me and walked through the house until she found him with this other woman. She cursed him and me and stormed out of the house, expressing loudly and clearly that she hoped Cole and I would both burn in hell. What a drama! Prime stuff for a talk show, I'm telling you." Quinton briefly grew silent. "I ran that skant of a woman out of my house and then I cursed Cole

28

out for being so stupid. He and I even went to blows that night before I put him out too, telling him where to go. We hadn't fought since we were kids fighting over points in a stupid pick-up basketball game." Quinton's expression turned remorseful. "You know, Dad, he and I never got a chance to make up or talk about that night. A few days later, I was back on the road and put Cole and his whorish ways out of my mind. The next thing I knew I got your long distance call, telling me he had been killed in that horrendous warehouse fire. Dad, Cole could drive me crazy, but I loved him like a brother. I tried my best to get him to do right by Angela." His lips thinned as though he were holding in his painful emotions. "Oh man, I hated losing him before we had a chance to set things right between us and Angela. To this day, she still believes I encouraged his infidelity."

Seeing how troubled Quinton was, Calvin placed his hand on his son's shoulder and smiled at him to bring him out of his funk. "What's done is done, son. Cole's death turned you around and away from that fast lifestyle I never approved of for you. I've watched you settle down and act responsibly the way a grown man should. I'm even more proud of you for that. You're going to make some woman a good husband. And that will be soon if your sister has any hand in it." He laughed softly, shaking Quinton's shoulder to get him out of the mood he was in.

Before anything else could be said, Quinton's sister

Jessica breezed into the kitchen. Her cinnamon face glowed with excitement and her eyes flashed with warmth when she spotted her brother. "Quinton, you finally made it," she declared with glee. "I only wish that Daddy's lady, Miss Beatrice, could have come too. She's going to be part of our family in a couple of weeks. It's too bad her sister had surgery and she had to go out of town to be with her." She grinned at her father. "We'll all be together though for your wedding which is fast approaching. Just think. We'll be one big happy family."

Calvin's eyes danced with merriment at the mention of the wedding. "There's nothing you like better than running your brother's and my business, is there, little lady?" .He glanced at his son. "My wedding has energized this girl. She and Beatrice are having the time of their lives with all the arrangements."

Jessica stood before the two men for whom she had abiding love and devotion. She had taken care of them since her mother had deserted them to live with a younger man whom she later married. The bond among the three of them was tight. No matter what went on in their lives, good or bad, they knew that they could count on one another for support. "I love happy occasions, especially for you guys. I'm so glad you've met a decent woman like Miss Beatrice," she said, staring at her father. " I'm looking forward to the wedding. Now if only I could get a decent woman for my brother to marry."

"See, what I mean, son." Calvin winked at Quinton. "Your brother is dating a hot number now. She could be the one," he told Jessica.

Jessica rolled her eyes impatiently. "Quinton, you can't be serious about Taylor Brown. She's barely out of high school. She and I have nothing in common. That won't work for me," she teased.

"She's twenty-two," Calvin spoke up for his son. "She's a cutie. And she can sing her young heart out. The kids all love her on BET and MTV."

"Daddy, what in the world do you know about videos?" Jessica gave her father a suspicious look.

"Hey, I'm down," he said. "I catch them when I cruise the channels with my remote. I watch the rump shaker videos. They're not all bad either." He broke into a laugh.

"Shame on you. Miss Beatrice will take care of all that soon enough," Jessica said, joining in his laughter. "I've watched Taylor Brown on those channels too. She is pretty and talented, but I don't think she's what Quinton needs. She may look like a woman in all those skimpy outfits she wears, but that girlfriend still has a lot of growing up to do from what she says when she's being interviewed. Quinton will be more like a father to her than a partner."

Quinton went and stood behind his sister. "I'm still here, you two. Taylor is a nice young woman. She and

Sinclair LeBeau

I are only dating right now. Nothing more."

Calvin took a seat on a stool at the kitchen bar to get a handful of the chocolate covered candy there. "Every time I pick up a copy of *Jet* or one of those grocery store newspapers I've seen pictures of you with her. You keep saying there's nothing between the two of you, but you and Taylor look pretty cozy. You keep hanging around and you'll get yourself into a lifetime commitment. A kid. You know those divas like Taylor don't mind having kids without getting married. I'd hate to have a grandson or granddaughter bought up with a father who's been treated like a stud."

"Yeah, Quinton, Daddy's right," Jessica said. "But then, Daddy, it can't be all that much to it. He hasn't brought her to Riley to meet us." She eyed Quinton, who had an amused look. "So you and I are worrying over nothing."

"I wish he would. I'd love to meet her," Calvin said. "I'm thinking of going out and buying her album. She sings some good stuff. It's reminds me of the R& B I listened to when I was a teenager myself."

"Dad, you don't have to buy her records. I'll get them for you and have her autograph them too." There was a mischievous twinkle in Quinton's eyes.

"Well, do that for me, son. I'll be a big hit with my friends," he chuckled.

Jessica said, "Quinton, you got to bring your little friend home for us to meet."

"Will do," Quinton said. "Just as soon as she has a break in her busy schedule." Taylor Brown, the latest pop diva, was an alluring woman. The two of them had met at a charity event in New York and had been dating occasionally. They had spent several weekends together in her mansion in L.A. Though Taylor's public image showed her as being sweet and sensitive, he had discovered her to be self-absorbed and caught up in the attention her fame and success had given her. Growing up poor, she was thrilled by all that she had achieved with her singing. With her newfound celebrity, she also relished the fact that she was sought after by high fashion designers to wear and model their expensive clothes. Designers were crazy for her exotic looks and the urban flair she brought to their fashions. Also, was the kind of woman who let you know exactly what was on her mind. She had let him know that she wanted him and wasted no time in expressing her feelings. Taylor was gorgeous and sexy and he certainly hadn't turned down what she so willingly offered. He had no deep feelings for Taylor. He enjoyed the sex with her and nothing more. As far as he was concerned, Taylor had a lot of growing up to do. He wasn't interested enough to wait around for her to learn what was really important in life. However, he enjoyed being her escort to various functions. He had made it clear that he liked her, but wasn't in love with her. Caught up in the swirl of her red hot career, Taylor couldn't comprehend any man not wanting her. So, she continued to treat him as though what they shared was something more. And because he had no one else special in his life, he hung around and reaped the pleasures of her attention and affection. Taylor was using him and he was using her. That was the way things went when two people were as high profile as they were. And for right now, their relationship was enough for him. She kept him from being lonely.

"Okay guys, enough about Taylor. I came to help my Stacey celebrate her birthday and not to have you two dabble into my personal life," Quinton said.

"You're right. This isn't the time to go into all of this celebrity gossip with the other room full of hyped kids," she said. "But I'm tired of seeing you hanging out with these vacuous minded bronze beauties who just want to be in your company because of your celebrity or the kind of money you're worth."

Quinton walked over to his sister and gave her a playful bear hug. "I'm a big boy, sis. I can look out for myself. And all of them aren't after my money. My dear Taylor is quickly catching up to me financially. The critics love her. She has a crossover appeal that is going to make her a very wealthy woman. Studios have begun to send her movie scripts. Hmm...I need to reconsider my feelings for her. I think I could get used to being a kept man by a sexy young thing like her." He chuckled and planted a wet kiss on her forehead, teasing her.

"Yuk," Jessica declared, feigning disgust and shoving him away. "You need to talk to your son, Daddy. Don't let him ruin his life with this Taylor sensation. I've got a feeling she won't be good for him."

Calvin laughed at his adult kids' actions. "When I was a young man, I never wanted a woman who was good for me."

Jessica grunted. "See, now you two are taking sides and trying to wreck my nerves."

Quinton laughed. "C'mon, Jessica. Enough about me. Today is my sweet niece's day. I've gotten her a gift that's going to make me the hero today." He pointed to the corner where he had placed his oversized package.

Jessica's eyes widened with delight. "Oh Quinton. You're going to spoil Stacey rotten with all your lavish gifts," she said in a chiding but loving tone.

Quinton smiled. "That's my angel. I got her a computer. It's time she had one," Quinton replied. "I've gotten her some neat games and programs on her level too. She is going to learn so much on that thing."

Jessica's stood near the package and looked as though she wanted to tear away all the colorful paper to inspect the item. "Doggone you, man. Her daddy and I were going to wait until next year but..."

"Too bad," Quinton said. "I've taken care of it. I'm good at buying affection," he teased. "She and I can have good times playing the games I bought her."

Jessica rushed up to her brother and embraced him to thank him for the gift. "Brother Que, you're too much.

Thanks." Her eyes danced from her gratitude. "It's time to serve the cake and ice cream. Light those candles, Quinton. I want you to bring out the cake. And Daddy, you come on too. You've hid out in this kitchen long enough. The kids aren't going to harm you," she assured him. "Eat some peppermint, Dad, so no one can smell the beer you've been sneaking out here. I'm supposed to be a perfect mom who has the perfect family," she said in a cheery tone.

Her father sighed and threw up his hands in exasperation. "I'm coming. But I want you both to watch my back. Those kids are loaded up with junk food and pretty hyped. No telling what's going to go down with them after they get to eat that fancy sugar-filled birthday cake and all that candy you have waiting for them in those goody bags you haven't served yet."

Jessica giggled at her father. "Stacey's friends aren't that bad." She went to the fridge and pulled down two gallons of ice cream. "Daddy, grab those paper plates and those plastic forks. Come on. Move it," she ordered.

Quinton and his father feigned annoyed looks.

"Daddy, I'm supposed to be a celebrity. People cater to me and don't order me around." He laughed.

Calvin laughed with him. "When you visit your sister, you know you have to leave your precious ego at the door. You're always going to be her little brother, the one she helped me keep in check while you both were growing up."

"Exactly," Jessica said, clutching the containers of ice cream and beckoning her father and brother with a nod of her head to move it.

With the lit candles on the cake, Quinton headed for the door that led to the other room. "Someone hold open the door for 'Sweet Que.'"

"I've got it, son," his father said. "Let's get this show on the room, so Jessica can give us some peace."

Jessica followed them. "Quinton, I want you to find a *nice* woman. The kind to settle down with and make a good home for you. Your niece needs some cousins."

Calvin chuckled at his daughter and patted his son sympathetically on his back for the warning words his sister had given him.

"Mercy, please don't start on that." Quinton sounded frustrated.

"I'm afraid that if you wait any longer to get married and have kids, you're going to end up feeling like a grandfather to them." She laughed.

Quinton looked amused. "So what if I might be too old to play with my kids or to lift them? You'll still have that chance to be an aunt." He hustled through the door to keep her from having the last word as she did most of the time.

During the remainder of the party, Quinton stood in the background of the dining room and watched his niece Stacey while her friends gathered around the cake to sing happy birthday to her. Standing with his arms folded, his mind drifted to a birthday party he had helped Angela with for Tyson when he had turned nine. This was a time when she was cool with his friendship with Cole. Cole had just gotten on at the fire station a few months earlier and he couldn't get off. He had asked Quinton to help Angela. It was at this time that Quinton learned that Cole and Angela were having serious martial problems. When Tyson's party had ended and the guests had left, leaving only him and Angela to clean up, he had found Angela in the kitchen with tears in her eyes. Quinton thought something had happened during the party to upset her. Concerned he had questioned her tears instead of ignoring them.

In between sobs, she revealed, "Cole doesn't love me, Quinton. He loves his son, but he's never really loved me. All of these years, I've done everything I could to make him love me. Nothing works. He acts as though our marriage is a prison. I know the only reason he has been with me for so long is because of Tyson. He'll do anything for that child. I feel like an outsider in my own home." She had bowed her head and cried.

Quinton remembered how her heartrending tears had filled him with mixed emotions. He had noticed himself how Cole had become a shameless flirt. He had even chastised his married friend for the way he had been coming on to women when the two of them would go out on the town for drinks or to play pool. In an effort to appease her fears, Quinton had gone to Angela and cupped her chin. He gazed into her teary brown eyes and studied her lovely face. In a flash his emotions of friendship turned into an attraction that he knew he had no business feeling. In that moment, he had wished that this woman who was his friend's wife could be his. He drew his hand away from Angela's face and jammed it into the pocket of his jeans and stepped back.

His heart raced but he managed an encouraging smile. "You're getting worked up about nothing. Cole is devoted to his family," he lied to make her feel better. "Maybe you're getting the wrong message from him. I mean, from what I've heard of couples who have been married as long as you two, I understand that relationships become comfortable and a bit of the romance cools. But it doesn't mean that there is no love." He felt foolish trying to convince her of something he had no knowledge of. He only wanted to comfort her and to see her smile again.

Angela wiped her eyes with the back of her hand. "I wish I could believe that. But Cole hasn't...hasn't touched me in nearly six months and..."

Quinton felt his neck growing warm with embarrassment. He was hearing way more than he wanted to hear. "Hey, maybe Cole is under a lot of stress at the firehouse. He's only been there for what...about six months. He's the first black there and I know it can't be easy for him. He's told me that he feels as though he was hired as a token. He's been anxious to show the other guys there that he is more than capable of handling the responsibilities and challenges of a firefighter. Give him some time. I'm sure you'll find out whatever is going on with him has nothing to do with you."

Angela considered what he said. Her eyes shifted nervously; she turned away from him and walked over to the dishwasher to fill it with dishes. "You're right. Maybe I'm making a big deal out of nothing." She glanced over her shoulder briefly and made an effort to smile, though it didn't reflect in her eyes. Quinton's heart swelled with sympathy. Though she put up a good front, he sensed that what he had said hadn't given her any consolation. He yearned to take her in his arms and to hold her near him to soothe her insecurities and relieve the loneliness she had been suffering.

Being a firefighter's wife couldn't be easy. Cole was often away from home for days on duty. And when he was off duty, he was out with him or took time to come to his pro games out of town. Quinton now felt guilty for paying for his friend's flights and giving him tickets to his games. When he had done this, he had never given any consideration to Angela's feelings or the fact that he was causing strife within their marriage. Quinton had assumed that everything was cool with her. After all, she knew how close he and Cole had been all of their lives.

Quinton swept the kitchen floor. As he worked, he eyed Angela, who was busy on the other side of room wrapping and putting away the leftover food from the party. He imagined what it would be like to be married to a woman as sweet and caring as he had witnessed Angela being to Cole. Though he was a pro athlete and had fame and fortune, he'd never experienced a meaningful relationship. He had had plenty of sex. There had been gorgeous women clamoring for his attention, but he knew they were only thinking of the things he could give them. When he had gotten into the NBA, he had been thrilled by all the easy women who offered themselves to him. He took pride in scoring with the models, the recording stars and the starlets who'd sought his attention fervently. However, he'd grown tired of the beauties with their agendas to share his bank account, his celebrity. After the momentary pleasure of sex, he wound up feeling used, empty and depressed. He wanted a real relationship, real love with a woman and not just erotic escapades that made him feel like a sex machine.

Angela broke Quinton out of his thoughts. "I didn't get a chance to see those pictures you took during Tyson's party with your Polaroid," she said in a much cheerier tone. "Get the pictures and we can relax in the living room. I'll pour us a nice glass of wine, so we can enjoy a snack. We deserve it after all the work we've done with the kids."

Quinton was pleased to see that Angela had composed herself. He welcomed the chance to spend more time with her. His heart had hummed with joy that evening when he was alone with his friend's lovely wife.

Sinclair LeBeau

For the next hour, he and Angela sat on the sofa going through the many humorous and adorable pictures he had taken with his instant camera of Tyson and his friends. Tyson's friends had been awed by "Sweet Quinton's" presence. Quinton had taken pictures with several of the partygoers and autographed the pictures he had taken. Angela had been impressed that Quinton had done such a generous thing for Tyson. She knew how he guarded his privacy and felt threatened when people came at him to use his celebrity in any way.

When Angela and Quinton were done laughing and going through the many snapshots, Quinton knew that he had to get away from his friend's wife. He was looking at her as a woman whom he wanted to really get to know on an intimate level. And he was ashamed of himself for having these feelings for the wife of his best friend. The several glasses of wine they had had relaxed him and intensified his sensitivity to her touch and her smile. Handing pictures back and forth with their shoulders touching and staring at her fresh-scrubbed face close to his had set off erotic sensors. It took everything in him to keep from stealing a kiss from her marvelous lips, or layering her elegant neck with kisses.

To quell these thoughts, Quinton scooted away from her and leaned over to take a special picture out of the pile. "May I have this picture?" he asked. It was one of her and Tyson and him taken by one of the parents who had helped out for a while.

42

Angela smiled with beautiful candor. "Sure. Take it," she insisted.

Quinton shot to his feet and prepared to leave to keep from doing something that would alienate Angela. "Thanks. I'm going to frame this and place it on the mantel in my apartment out of town to remember this day. It'll show my homeboys my sensitive side." Suddenly he felt awkward and hoped that Angela couldn't read the sinful thoughts that were going on his mind. "I really enjoyed being with the kids. They really ran us ragged for awhile, didn't they? You know Cole had to beg me," he admitted. "I was skeptical about being here. I just couldn't see myself babysitting with a bunch of eight and nine-year-olds. But I had fun. In fact, it's one of the best times I've had in quite some time."

Smiling, Angela stood and stretched, revealing how tired she was.

Quinton groaned silently, watching her reach her arms above her head. She let out a soft grunt that shifted his imagination to a sexual fantasy. And he couldn't help noticing the way her perfectly shaped breasts lifted and fell, causing his hands to ache to touch them.

"Excuse me," she said, tugging down her top that had risen to show off her flat tummy, trim waist. She ran her fingers through her shiny, raven hair that had lost its curl from her busy party activities. She reached out and took Quinton by the hand. "Thanks so much for putting up with all the confusion. Though his dad couldn't be here, I know Tyson will never forget this birthday. And he loves that fancy digital watch you gave him. He loves the fact that it's waterproof. I know he's going to take a bath in it the first chance he gets to see just how much water it can take." She laughed softly.

Quinton was mesmerized by the delightful sound of her laughter. He wished he could think of a reason to draw his visit out longer. Instead, he did the gentlemanly thing and headed for the front door with her following close behind him. He stopped at the door and turned and stared at Angela, who was a captivating vision with her eyes a bit drowsy and her hair mussed. His heart raced and his mouth grew dry from the erotic thoughts that went straight from his mind to his maleness. He swallowed hard. "Good night, Angela," he said in a quiet tone. He leaned down and placed a brief, gentle kiss on her forehead. Touching his lips to the warm flesh of her forehead, he closed his eyes to relish the jolt of tenderness he experienced. He struggled with himself to keep from enfolding her in his arms and crushing her to him. He was flooded with emotion when she reached up and hugged him the way a grateful friend would. She murmured her thanks once again and released him.

Ever since that day of Tyson's party, Quinton had found himself fantasizing and dreaming of his best friend's wife. He wanted a woman like her for himself. But he believed that God had broken the mold when it came to good, loving women like Angela. When Cole was alive, he didn't visit Cole's house when he knew his buddy wasn't there because of his secret crush. And when Cole was home and he visited, he kept his socialization with her to a minimum. He harbored a secret desire that he knew could wreck a valued friendship. But now that Cole was deceased, he had begun to think of Angela in romantic terms again. However, there were Tyson's feelings to consider. He would have to share Angela with her son, who meant the world to her. Was the boy ready or mature enough to let his mother have a relationship and a bit of happiness for herself? he wondered.

"Quinton, son." Calvin slapped his son on the back. "You must be thinking of ways to make more money," he teased. "Snap out of it. Your sister wants you and me to take pictures with Stacey and her friends around her cake before it's sliced."

Quinton wiped his hands over his eyes wearily as though he was trying to wipe away the emotions that reigned in his heart for Angela after all this time and everything they had been through. He realized he was a glutton for punishment. Angela didn't even want his friendship. She blamed him for breaking up her marriage. And then there were Tyson's feelings to consider. What would the boy think of his mother having a relationship with his father's best friend, a man whom he had thought of as an uncle at one time in his life? Quinton exhaled deeply. As a big time athlete, he had been used to getting whatever he wanted in life. But he had a feeling that Angela would laugh in his face if he dared to even hint at trying to get next to her. Unlike most women who were impressed by his celebrity, his money and his material things, she wasn't fazed at all. When Angela looked at him, all she saw was the guy who had been her husband's boyhood friend who had been fortunate enough to make it in a world that men like her husband could only dream about.

Quinton's melancholy reverie ended when he was poked in the ribs by his sister, urging him into position near Stacey. Quinton took his place beside Stacey and joined in singing happy birthday all the while thinking of Tyson's birthday party where he had fallen in love with another man's wife.

Chapter 3

B y the time Angela had closed her bookstore, All of Our Best, that crisp Friday the last week in October, she had decided to go see Quinton and to seek the help he had offered her for Tyson that day she had seen him in the mall. Driving to Quinton's popular sports bar, Quinton's Corner, she thought how earlier that day she had spent more than an hour at her son's middle school with the dean of students. She'd had to leave her store in the care of her college age employee in order to pick up Tyson, who had been suspended for an awful fight he had been involved in in the cafeteria. The altercation had been with some boy who had called Tyson a punk. The dean also had informed Angela that Quinton had been reported to the office by several of his teachers for insubordination on several occasions. Angela had been humiliated by her son's behavior. To her his actions were a reflection of his home training. And she had always prided herself on being a good mother. Because she had been so wrapped up in opening and running the bookstore since spring, she'd had no clue that Tyson had become so obnoxious. She felt guilty for being so consumed by her new business that she hadn't recognized change in her son. She had assumed that the timing for her to do something for herself like opening the store was perfect. After all, Tyson was no longer a little kid who needed her hovering over him and reminding him what he needed to do. He had assured her that he could look after himself until she got home from work. She had believed him and trusted him and thought that he was responsible enough to stay out of trouble while she worked to establish her business.

But she had misjudged her son. That mall situation and now the trouble in school had shown her that she had to keep a closer check on him. How dare she let the store make her forget that her main priority was her growing son's well-being? she chided herself. She loved Tyson with all her heart and the thought of him wasting himself unnerved her. His behavior reminded her of what kids did when they had been neglected by their parents. And she certainly didn't want to be considered a bad parent. She had always seen to it that Tyson had what he needed. But, lately she might have slipped in giving him the kind of attention he required. After working in her store all day, she was worn out. She'd drag home from the store by seven or eight o'clock in the evening and ask Tyson how his school day had been and whether he had done his homework. The boy would always tell her what she wanted to hear. And that was that he'd had an okay day and yes, his homework was done. Angela would be pleased, thinking that everything was fine and then prepare a quick meal for them. They'd talk briefly about their chores and plans for the next day and then the two of them would retire to their bedrooms for the night.

She'd assumed that if Tyson had any problems that he would share them with her. He hadn't mentioned any trouble, so she figured that he was getting along fine in school. She was disgusted with herself for being clueless to her son's trouble.

Even though the bookstore had been a distraction to her relationship with Tyson, she vowed to pay more attention to what was going on at home. She could be in business and still run her household. Now that she had a taste of being a business woman, she didn't want to give it up. Opening up the bookstore, had been a panacea to all the heartache and loneliness she had known. Up until this time, she had felt insignificant. There had been the humiliation of knowing that Cole was a hopeless philanderer. Then he died, leaving her alone with Tyson. Just as she was recovering from that situation, the following year her father died from a massive heart attack that floored her mother, her sister, and herself. Angela had

had enough of sadness and trouble. Her venture into the book business had given her a sense of comfort and gratification. The planning and the hard work she had placed into All of Our Best had lifted her out of the depression she had experienced from her losses and her bruised ego in the last few years. But how could she enjoy her success when her child was getting himself into so much trouble?

It was because of this that Angela decided that tonight would be the best night for her to go talk with Quinton. She hadn't called Quinton at his business to let him know that she was coming. She was afraid that she might lose her nerve if she called ahead of time. She was just going on faith by showing up at his place and hoping that he would have the time to talk.

Tyson would be spending the night and weekend with his grandmother and great aunt who lived together. A friend of the Etheridges, his grandmother and maiden aunt, taught at Tyson's middle school and this person had wasted no time in rushing to Cole's relatives with the news of Tyson's hoodlum behavior. Although Miss Viveca, Cole's mother, and Aunt Nadine, his aunt, hadn't verbalized their feelings, Angela knew that the women blamed her newly established business and long working hours for the problems Tyson was having. When they had first learned what she planned on doing with part of the money she had received from her husband's insurance money and benefits as a firefighter, she'd had to assure them that she hadn't squandered all of the money on the business, that she had set aside money for Tyson's education and future.

Angela knew that the ladies who had reared her husband were certain that she was making a big mistake by venturing into a business on her own. Yet, Angela had already done quite well in her quaint African-American bookstore. The Blacks in the community had been hungry for a place that specialized in books by and about Blacks. All of Our Best was drawing a steady clientele of voracious Black readers. Having a business and being considered a professional had given her a sense of confidence she'd never felt before or ever dreamed of having. That feeling validated the self-worth that her years of marriage had taken from her. It had been her love of books that had given her the idea for the store. Her reading had sustained her during the lonely years of her marriage to Cole and even after his death when she was all alone with a son to raise.

Reaching the nearly full parking lot at Quinton's Corner, Angela noticed that many of the customers who entered were men. She assumed that this was a favorite hangout for those who liked ogling young women dressed in clingy satin uniforms that resembled basketball cheerleader outfits.

The moment that Angela strolled inside the place, she caught several men studying her as though they wanted to make a move on her. The thought unnerved her. She made her way to the nearest vacant table and opened a menu to wait for a waitress, so she could ask for Quinton.

Suddenly there were hoots and howls over the score of a football game that blasted on the theater-sized television in the sports bar. Looking around the crowded bar, she saw no signs of Quinton. She had seen his shiny black utility vehicle, a Lexus jeep bearing Que #1 vanity plates in the lot. Annoyed by the noise and the men who kept eyeing her as though they thought she was looking for male companionship, she was relieved when a waitress finally appeared at her table.

"Hi, welcome to Quinton's Corner. What will you have today?" the waitress asked in a perky tone.

With a hint of a smile, Angela looked at the young woman. "I'll order later. I'd really like to speak with Quinton Gibbs."

A glimmer of interest and a smile tilted the waitress's mouth. "I see. We get that request a lot. He's busy right now and..."

Angela didn't like the patronizing look the waitress gave her. "I happen to be a...a friend of Quinton," she explained, giving the woman a cool look. "Tell him that Angela Etheridge is here, please."

"Sure thing, lady," the waitress with the name tag that read Krystal said, wheeling around on the heels of her sneakers and heading toward the back of the restaurant and through an employees door.

Angela settled back in her chair with her hands folded and focused her attention on the view outside the plate glass window. Growing impatient for Quinton's appearance, she turned her attention back to what was going in the restaurant. She caught a bald, middle-aged man staring at her. He grinned and winked. She groaned silently and opened the menu, pretending to study it.

Thankfully, the perky waitress returned to the table, beaming. "You're in luck. Quinton says he'll be with you in a minute. He's taking a long distance call right now," she said. "He told me to serve you whatever you wanted while you waited. It's on the house."

"Bring me a diet cola," Angela requested. Her mouth had grown dry from anxiety, thinking of the reason she had come to talk with Quinton.

"It's yours," the Kystal said, swishing away to get her order.

Waiting for her drink and Quinton, she wondered if he was talking with that young singing sensation that she had seen him escorting in the magazines. Taylor Brown. She was light complexioned with lustrous, long honey blonde hair. She was always scantily dressed. Tyson was enamored of the young singer. He and his buddies thought the young woman was a goddess. Thinking of Quinton's relationship with this young pop star, Angela wondered if she was making the right decision by bringing Quinton into her son's life. Maybe he wouldn't have time for Tyson. Assessing Quinton's business, she also wondered if it was a reflection of his lifestyle. To her the place seemed geared toward horny men. Shapely, pretty young waitresses, theater-sized televisions that blasted sports events, and all the beer and tasty high cholesterol food a soul could want. Quinton had the money-making formula working.

The waitress served Angela her drink with a smile and dashed off to wait on a table of rowdy men who had just arrived and addressed her by name. Seeing the men leer and flirt with the young woman made Angela think of her husband. She knew that when Cole traveled to be with Quinton when he was in the pros that they hung out in places like this one. There was no doubt in her mind that her husband probably acted as obnoxious over girls as these men. Her depressing memory was interrupted by the sudden appearance of Quinton.

Quinton flashed his perfectly aligned white teeth that complemented his creamy chocolate complexion. "Angela, I can't believe you've finally come to what I imagine you think is my den of sin," he said with a hint of mischief. He dropped his long form onto the chair in front of her.

Warmed by his smile, she matched it. "Neither can I," she deadpanned. "Quite a bit of lecherous action around here. I just hope the place doesn't get struck down by a bolt of lightning because of the overload of lustful thoughts in here," she teased.

Quinton laughed, sincerely amused. "That's a good

54

one. But it's harmless in here. It's just a place where fellows can come and relax and feel like real men. There's nothing sinful going on in here. This is a class operation, lady. I wouldn't hang my name on anything that's sleazy." He sat forward and rested his arms on the table. "I'd like to think you've stopped by to say hello. But I dare to dream. Your visit is about Tyson, right?"

Her expression dimmed and she nodded. "I'm afraid so." She sighed. "I don't know what to do with him. I had to go pick him up from school today. He's been put out for a couple of days for fighting." Her brow furrowed. "And while I was there I learned about some other trouble he's been involved in. I discovered that my son has been disrespectful to his teachers and not even making an effort to do his school work." She held the sides of her face and breathed deeply as though she were going through that humiliating conversation with the dean of students again.

Quinton sat back in his chair and crossed his legs. He considered Tyson's situation. Angela didn't deserve what that boy was putting her through. Hadn't Cole given her enough hell in his last days? he mused. "Listen, it's going to work out," he said, offering her encouragement. "Tyson is having growing pains. He's at that age where he feels he has to prove he's a man. The only thing is, he's going about it in all the wrong ways. He's taking advantage of you and your love for him. He knows there is only so much you're going to do to him. And he can charm you with his promises of doing better. If Cole was alive, he wouldn't even dare to think about the junk he's gotten himself into."

Angela folded her arms at her waist and considered Quinton's words. Being able to talk with him and to share her problems gave her some relief. "You're right. Cole and I had our problems, but he knew how to keep Tyson in line." She grew pensive and sad, thinking how ironic it was for Cole to love their son but to be without passion when it came to her. She had punished herself over that issue and still hadn't been able to let go of the way she had suffered in her marriage in order to pretend to have a happy home for Tyson.

Quinton caught the look of sadness in Angela's eyes. "He was better with Tyson than with anyone else in his life. He was proud to have a son. He had big dreams and plans for Tyson's future."

With a distant look in her eyes, Angela ran a hand through her hair and let her arm rest on the back of her chair. Sitting in this manner revealed the lush curve of her breasts. She caught Quinton's eyes lingering there and she grew self-conscious. Dropping her arm, she sat up straight. "Just this afternoon, I reminded Tyson of how much his father wanted for him. But the child tuned me out. My conversations involving his father make him defensive and withdraw into himself." She looked concerned. "I know he's afraid to admit that he misses and needs his dad. I'm an adult and I certainly miss my father since he passed. I've tried to share my own feelings about death with him and to let him know I understand how he feels. I've tried to be there for him, but I'm learning that I can't fill the role of mother and father. I'm not the superwoman I thought I could be. Until recently, I thought my love for Tyson would be enough to help him get past the loss of his father and help him grow up."

Quinton listened carefully. He wanted to share the personal experiences that he had in common with Tyson. He understood somewhat how Tyson felt. When his mother up and left their family when he was about Tyson's age, he had missed her terribly. She had left him feeling confused and hurt. Although his father had done his best to carry on and made every effort to show his kids that everything was all right, it didn't make up for the love and attention he yearned for from his mother who he felt had betrayed him by running off. She hadn't died, but a young Quinton had grieved her betrayal, desertion as though she had. "I was sorry to hear about your father. Someone who knew you passed that bit of information on to me," he said in a quiet voice. "It's rough, isn't it? Losing a parent any kind of way can be tough," Quinton said, pushing down the old hurts that welled up in his heart from his past. "You and I will figure out how to help Tyson," he assured her. He was going to find a way to help Tyson deal with his feelings. He didn't want the boy to have to struggle with feelings of inadequacy the way he had.

His words filled Angela with optimism. "I hoped you meant what you said to me that day. I know that you have a lot going on in your life. It's kind of you to take time for us. My father did what he could with Tyson. But holidays and a few visits during the year weren't enough. It's difficult to help a child when there are so many miles between you."

Quinton nodded with understanding. "By the way how are your mother and sister?" He smiled. "They're doing better. My sister married a guy in the air force. They're stationed in Germany for the next couple of years. And she's expecting their first child. My mother is over there with her. My sister has some complications with this first pregnancy. The doctor wants her to have bed rest, so, my mother is there with her helping out to make sure she will go full-term. I talk to them long distance often, but I still miss them. I haven't seen them since spring."

"So, you're all on your own," he said, studying her.

"Exactly," she responded. "I suppose that's why these issues with Tyson have overwhelmed me so badly."

Quinton stared at her warmly. "You're not alone anymore. I meant what I told you that day in the mall, Angela. I'm glad that you've finally come to me. I'm sure that together we can get Tyson in line."

She smiled and her almond complexion glowed. "I certainly hope so."

He liked the glow of relief on her lovely face. It lit

her eyes, erased her brow of worry and turned that wonderful mouth into a display of joy. Pleased that she had come to him, Quinton was more than willing to be a part of Tyson's life and hers. Knowing that Angela blamed him for her husband's infidelities, he was anxious to eradicate the negative impression she had formed of him over the years. In the beginning Quinton had cloaked a few of Cole's one night stands with other women. Older and wiser now, he knew he'd been wrong for being such a cohort to Cole's wrongdoings. Cole had been a lucky man who had foolishly risked the treasure of a loving family–a devoted wife and a wonderful son.

Quinton stared at Angela. "I'm here for you and Tyson. You can take that to the bank," he vowed.

Angela let her head fall back in a display of elation and her brown eyes grew even more vibrant. She placed her hand over her heart and swallowed as though she were fighting back her emotions. "I really appreciate your support, Quinton," she said in a soft and appreciative tone. "Goodness, that son of mine of is aging me."

Quinton looked amused by her admission. "You don't look like a woman who's worn with worry. You look great," he said, smiling. He wanted to tell her she looked more like Tyson's older sister than his mother. But he didn't want Angela to think that he was putting her on with the kind of lines he used to get close to women while playing the game.

Angela's face grew warm and she could no longer

look into his piercing eyes. She shifted in her seat, feeling affected by his good looks and his kindness. Before she could think of anything to continue their conversation, one of the waitresses came to their table for Quinton.

She placed her hand on his shoulder and smiled broadly. "Mr. Que, I hate to disturb you. We have some guys here who would like for you to take a few pictures with them. They have deep pockets, boss. They are promising to donate some big money to your scholarship fund. All they want is a chance to talk to you and to get autographs and pictures."

Quinton's honey-colored eyes flashed with enthusiasm. With a cordial expression, he rose from his chair with a grace that accentuated his exquisite athletic form. He placed his hand on Angela's shoulder and stared down at her. "Don't leave. I'll be back in a few minutes." Then he strolled away.

Feeling heat where he had touched her, Angela rolled her shoulders slightly. The sensation was an unexpected response. She watched him walk up to the men who had beckoned him and greet them with that fabulous charm that was part of his personality, his success as a superstar athlete.

Taking a sip of her soft drink, Angela tried not to think of Quinton in terms of being sexy and handsome. She wanted to think of him as just Quinton, the guy who had been her husband's friend. But now that she had been alone and on her own and hadn't seen Quinton in the last few years, she found herself viewing him the way any average woman would. The man was electrifying, she admitted to herself. His creamy chocolate complexion, his bright and quick smile were dynamite. His six-foot-four frame was well-toned and looked great in the designer jeans he wore with a tan colored sweater. He had that thing. That charisma. She understood why he had several commercial endorsements for credit cards, soft drinks and even computers. And she could understand why Taylor Brown, the pop diva, wanted him for herself.

Angela found herself smiling with admiration at Quinton with his adoring fans. Who would have thought that a boy who had grown up in Riley, Virginia, had been deserted by his mother and raised by a father who owned and operated a neighborhood grocery store would have turned into such a prince of a man? she mused. The first few years that he had gone pro, Quinton had become a bit obnoxious and wild. The flashy cars, the big houses, the glamorous women, and partying with celebrities had become an integral part of his life. It was this lifestyle that her husband had envied and squeezed his way into. Cole had taken great pride not only in being Quinton's friend, but a friend to Quinton, "Sweet Que," the millionaire celebrity. It wasn't until he had hurt his knee and became disabled that Quinton finally got his priorities straight, Angela thought. It was then that he seemed to look around to see how he could use his celebrity to help others. Although she hadn't had contact with him, she had read in the papers and magazines about his charitable deeds to youth. Now he lived the kind of life that a young boy should want to mimic, she decided. What he did or whom he dated was none of her concern. Regardless, she was glad that he was offering his time to help her get Tyson back on the right track.

As soon as Quinton had satisfied the customers with his presence and had begun to make his way back to her table, he was surrounded by another small group of admirers who sought chitchat and autographs. He obliged each person with a cheerful word and a smile. "Sorry about the intrusion. I can't ever turn down anyone who is willing to contribute to my scholarship fund for the community. Those guys are lawyers from Norfolk who drove in to check out my place. They have deep pockets. They gave me generous checks for the kids in my program." He patted his shirt pocket where he had placed the checks, then signaled for a waitress who wasted no time getting to him. "Bring me a beer, sweetheart," he ordered with a drop-dead smile. Before the pretty college age woman could rush off, he snagged her by the wrist to hold her still. "You want a fresh soda or a sandwich?" he asked Angela. "It's on the house."

Angela said, "No thanks. I'm fine."

Watching Quinton sip on his beer, Angela was anxious to set up a schedule with Quinton for Tyson. She didn't want to rush him, but she couldn't bear the thought of her son getting involved in any more trouble.

He must have read her mind. He reached over and touched her hand in a caring manner. "I'd like to get with Tyson soon. Fortunately, my schedule is clear for the next few weeks. I don't have to go out of town for anything. Most of my business can be handled right from Riley. If you can give me a time that is convenient for you, we can get started with Tyson as soon as possible."

The moment his hand touched hers, her heart skipped a beat. Feeling flustered, she moved her hand and used it to brush her bangs to the side. However, she liked his take charge attitude. It filled her with even more confidence about Tyson. She gave him a grateful look. "Can you have supper with us on Sunday?"

He contemplated her question briefly. "If you're cooking, I'm all yours," he said. "But, there's a big game that evening. We usually have a crowd and I like to be around for my customers."

"No problem. We'll eat early. Tyson should be in a better mood than he was the last time he saw you," she assured him.

"I certainly hope so. But don't make a big deal out of me coming. I'm a stranger to him. When you're not around, kids forget you so quickly. He and I are going to have to get to know each other all over again."

Angela felt a tinge of guilt. After all, she had been

the one to shut Quinton out of their lives. At the time, she had given no consideration to what effect taking Quinton out of his life would have on Tyson or for that matter Quinton. All she remembered was feeling betrayed and hurt by the way she believed Quinton had conspired with Cole to allow use of his place for his illicit love trysts.

"I sure hope so. You're my last hope, Quinton. His grandmother and great aunt are making hints that I'm an unfit mother. You know how old-fashioned they are about a woman's role in the home. You see, I've opened a bookstore, All of Our Best." She smiled proudly. "They haven't been at all happy with me starting my own business." The look of pride faded. "They think I'm selfish, foolish, and in over my head. Tyson's behavior has only validated the doubts they expressed to me concerning my staying home, so that I can monitor Tyson's every move."

Quinton shook his head and smiled like a Cheshire cat. "Good for you. I think it's great that you have your own thing. You shouldn't let Miss Viveca and her sister get to you. They are the last of the old school women. I know they must be in a tailspin over the problems that Tyson is having. I remember how they used to stay on Cole, trying to make him fit into the image of what they thought was a proper Black gentleman. Even though it was done out of love, Cole hated the social events they had him attending, trying to refine him. He was a happy brother when he graduated from high school and was able to live on campus away from his snooping mother and aunt."

"Those women are too much. I've tried to be patient with them and to stay close with them for Tyson's sake. After all, they are his blood relations. Tyson is all that they have left now that Cole is dead. I often feel as though the women only tolerate me because I'm Tyson's mother. I don't want to feel that way, but I do."

Quinton saw in Angela's eyes that sad look that always made him want to take her in his arms to comfort her. Cole had come from a prominent Black family in the community. His father had been a physician who had died with an aneurysm. His mother and maiden aunt had both been teachers and principals in the Riley school system. Cole had shattered the Etheridges' plans for him to be a doctor or lawyer. Cole had no interest in either. He wanted to be a pro athlete. To him that was everything. When he was in college, he spent most of his time partying and chasing as many women as he could. Angela had fallen for Cole's game and had gotten pregnant. His mother and aunt had been devastated that Cole had not only gotten a girl they considered a social outsider pregnant, but also that he had not done as well as he should in college. Cole had liked Angela but he had never been in love with her, Quinton knew.

Before they could continue their conversation, the waitress returned to serve Quinton his beer. He rewarded her with a smile and a squeeze on her arm.

Quinton was such a flirt, Angela thought. She noticed how the young woman blushed from his attention.

Quinton took a long swallow of brew. He stared at Angela with a twinkle in his eyes. "Tell me about this business of yours that's turning you into such a bad mother." He grinned. "I'd like to hear more about it now we've gotten the serious business cleared for now."

At the mention of her business, Angela's almond-colored complexion brightened. She sat tall and proud. "It's an African-American bookstore in a small shopping center near Sedgewick Mall. I opened it during the spring. Business has been wonderful since day one. Next to having Tyson, it's been the most exciting thing in my life."

His honey-colored eyes lingered on her lovely face and a smile tilted the corners of his mouth. "So you're the one who rented that site. I've been meaning to stop by there, but I've been extremely busy until now. I usually make an effort to visit all of my new tenants to wish them well."

Angela looked stunned. "Are you telling me that you own the shopping center?" She stared at him, revealing how shocked she was by the news. "I'm renting my business from you?"

Quinton nodded. "Yes, you are. But don't look so disturbed, Angela. I'm not an awful landlord."

"Well, I'm surprised. I had no idea you had a holding there." She ran her hand through her hair and looked as though she was trying to control herself.

"I bought that site a couple of years ago. It's been quite profitable. Your store makes that place even more special. There's a video store, a yogurt parlor, a sub shop and a beauty salon. No wonder you and the other tenants are doing so well. People can spend a nice afternoon or evening just going from store to store. There's plenty of business for everyone."

Angela was astonished by the information. How ironic was it for her to be doing business with a man whom she had vowed not to have anything to do with? He was becoming entangled in her life in more ways than one. He not only had agreed to mentor her son, but now she learned that her thriving place of business was being rented from him.

Quinton interrupted her thoughts by continuing their conversation. "I've got to get to your place now that I know you're running it. Since I've retired from the pros, I've become a voracious reader."

Angela gave him a dubious look. "You're putting me on, right? I mean, a big-time former athlete turned businessman who dates one of the most successful entertainers in the country can't possibly have any time to snuggle up with a book."

Giving her a slow, easy smile, Quinton said, "Taylor loves to read as much as I do. There is nothing she or I like to receive from one another better than a stack of the latest books by Black authors. And reading relaxes me, takes me out of myself and my problems. Is that something you can buy?" he asked, feeling mischievous.

"It's surprising, but doesn't sound like the Quinton I used to know, the one who loved to snuggle with whatever available woman was willing to get into bed with him," she said.

"That used to be me. I'm not like that anymore. I've been through a lot of things that have changed my life, my thinking. Despite what you've always chosen to believe about me and my lifestyle, I'm just an ordinary guy who wants the same thing any man wants."

Angela smirked at him, considering what most men like Quinton and her husband wanted from women.

"And it's not what you think," he said, reading the expression on her face. "I just want a woman who wants me for myself. A woman who can understand me, respect me and love me," he said, expressing himself in a tentative manner to see her reaction to his sensitive side.

"From what I've seen of pictures of you and Taylor splattered all over the glossy magazines, holding hands and giving each other *that look*, I suppose you've found what you're looking for in her."

Quinton hesitated before speaking. "Taylor is a nice person. I know she comes off as this sexy, designer-clothes-wearing woman, but there's a lot more to her. I admire her for the way she has managed to make a success of herself. She's a young woman who has come from a meager background. To look at the polished woman she's become you wouldn't know that only a few years ago she lived in a crummy neighborhood, barely surviving with her hard working parents and five other siblings. Taylor is a go-getter. His eyes glimmered as though he had been hit by some memory of a hot interlude between them.

"I'm happy for you. I really am," Angela said, wishing to end the discussion of his social life and his high praise for Taylor. She glanced at her watch. "It's late and I should be on my way. I've kept you from your business long enough." Smiling politely, she rose from her chair.

Quinton stood too. He grabbed her elbow and stared down at her, lavishing on her one of his dazzling smiles. "I'm really looking forward to being with Tyson again."

She averted her glance from his infectious smile and proceeded to head for the exit. "I really appreciate you taking an interest and spending your time with him."

Just as Angela arrived at the door, Quinton held her by the shoulder. "You don't know how much this will mean to me. It will be kind of healing for me to have the opportunity to be with Cole's son." He paused thoughtfully. "It's time for us to let go of the past for Tyson's sake," he said, looking earnest. "Don't you agree?"

She stared at him and smiled. "I suppose you're

right." She sighed with resignation. "Tyson's future is what is important now. I can't let him waste himself in any way. I can't stand by and let that happen." Her eyes flashed with anxiety. "I'll be in touch about the time to come to dinner." Pushing the glass door open to leave, she glanced over her shoulder to find Quinton watching her. She waved and smiled. Reaching her car, she felt buoyant. Never in her wildest dreams had she imagined that Quinton Gibbs, the one time bad boy of the NBA, of all people would be so willing take on the role of guardian angel to her child.

Chapter 4

"Hey, look at this picture in *Jet* of our Quinton Gibbs with Taylor Brown," exclaimed a young female customer to her friend at the magazine stand in All of Our Best.

Angela, who was nearby straightening out the rack of romance novels, stood close to the two college-aged girls and listened to their exchange over Quinton. "That Taylor is a lucky woman to have a fine brother like Quinton. Look at him in that tux," gushed one of the girls. "Doesn't he look like a million dollars?"

"He's worth a million dollars in more ways than one, girlfriend," the other girl said. Her voice dripped with admiration.

"Look at them. They are the perfect couple. She's gorgeous and talented and he's tall, dark and handsome," continued the first young woman.

"And paid," added the other girl. "I sure would like to be his woman. He looks as though he could make me some kind of happy. If you know what I mean." The first girl giggled. "I heard that! Look at how they are eyeing each other. They have the hots for one another girl. Just look at that fabulous hunk of man," she gushed. "Can't you tell he gives good lovin'?"

The girl snatched the magazine from her friend. "No doubt. Girl, look how Quinton is checking out the woman's bosom like every man who was at that affair probably was. That designer dress she has on barely covers her nipples. But she has the figure and looks to get away with it. I wonder if she glued or taped it to cover up her nipples." She snickered.

"You're too much. You turn everything into a dirty joke." The girl took the magazine and placed it back on the stand. "Pay for your book and let's go. I'm ready to eat at the sub shop next door..."

As the two young ladies went to the counter to check out with Christina, All of Our Best's only employee, Angela went to the magazine stand and picked up the issue of *Jet* that the girls had been reading. She thumbed through the magazine until she found the picture that had intrigued the two girls and she studied the picture of Quinton with his arm around Taylor Brown. The two looked elegant attending some charity event in New York, according to the caption. They also looked as though they had cozy feelings for each other, Angela thought. She closed the magazine and slapped it back on the shelf. Good for Quinton, she thought. He needed someone who was a celebrity like himself. This Taylor person had had two chart-topping albums in the last three years. Both had been nominated for music awards. Taylor had just as much money as Quinton. So, she obviously wasn't interested in the type of material things Quinton could buy her like some of the other women who tried to capture him with their snares.

"It's closing time," Christina reminded her boss. "I have a date tonight," added the college senior, beaming with excitement. Christina had been bubbly for the last month. She had finally met a guy that really made her happy at last, she'd confided in Angela.

Angela smiled at the young girl who she could see was anxious to get away from the store and hurry home to prepare for her evening out. "Help me straighten and replace some of these books back on the shelves and you may leave. I won't make you run the vacuum tonight, Cinderella," she teased.

"Thanks, boss lady," Christina said, grinning. She turned on the radio that was kept behind the counter.

An upbeat song ended and then the DJ gave an intro for the latest Taylor Brown ballad. The sensual melody flooded the store. She sang a soulful account of the joys of her precious love. Christina hustled from behind the counter, singing loudly off key the words to the song as she busied herself completing her chores.

Angela cringed at Christina's singing. "That's a nice song. You really like it, huh?" Christina placed her hand on her heart and nodded, grinning as though she didn't want to be bothered while listening to the record.

Angela was amused by Christina's intensity. She straightened some books that had been left disheveled. Listening to the song, Angela was touched by the emotion in Taylor's voice. It was obvious in her song that the younger woman had experienced the joys of love. Angela became nostalgic remembering her first and only romance. The one she had shared with Cole. Her love for him had been precious and sweet. She had done everything in her power to be the kind of woman he could love and treasure. But no matter what she had done, it had never been enough. She had spent most of her married life being lonely and hurt by her husband's rejection of her love, the love she wanted to be special. Since his death, she hadn't considered another relationship. She had been drained emotionally by all that she had been through in her marriage before her husband's untimely death. With his infidelities, then his death, her hopes and dreams of what real love was had been shattered. She simply didn't have the energy or courage to love that way again. She had sublimated all her energy into making a success of her store, All of Our Best. Before she had the store and before she learned how unfaithful her husband was, she had been quite happy as housewife and a mother. Keeping a house and taking care of her two favorite guys had been enough. But once she started to suspect her husband's interests in other women, she grew restless and wanted more for herself than cooking and cleaning to make his life easier. She had been hurt that her efforts at a happily-ever-after marriage had failed. However, she continued to be a good mother. Her son would always need her and love her unconditionally. It was the one thing in her life that gave her comfort when she realized that she was in love alone in her marriage. After Cole's death, she had mentioned to her parents her desire for a store. They had urged her to follow through with the idea. So, in the months after her husband's death, she sought advice from small business counselors who helped her fulfill her ambition of owning a bookstore. With her business, she had gotten a lot of satisfaction from feeling independent and being successful.

"Oh I love that Taylor Brown!" Christina gushed when the song ended. "She is the lady. I wish they would play it one more time."

By the time Christine had completed the task that Angela had asked of her, her boyfriend had pulled up outside of the store. She grabbed her coat and purse and asked Angela what time she wanted her to come to work on Monday. Angela had barely gotten the time out before Christine called good-night and was out the door to hurry home to prepare for her date.

Alone in the store, Angela locked the door and waited for Tyson to return with Quinton from the football game. She wandered over to the magazine stand and picked up the copy of *Jet* once again to get another glimpse of Quinton with Taylor. This time she ignored Taylor and studied Quinton. Just for a brief moment, she wondered what her life would have been like if she had chosen to go out with Quinton instead of Cole when she had met the two her freshman year at college. She remembered that she had been drawn to Quinton who at the time was a skinny, shy and sweet boy who hung around with the outgoing and handsome Cole. But Cole with his great looks and charm had made her quickly dismiss any romantic thoughts she had of Quinton.

Noticing the sight of approaching headlights, Angela returned the magazine to its place and banished her thoughts of what could have been. Quinton's jeep wheeled into a parking spot right in front of her store. Angela removed the striped apron she wore while she worked and went to unlock the door for Quinton and Tyson. She held it open for them, letting in the breezy November air.

Tyson hustled up to his mother and hooked his arm with hers. "Mom, we're going to a wedding," he announced enthusiastically.

"Say what?" Angela replied with interest, remembering the picture of Quinton and Taylor in the magazine she had just placed back.

Quinton strolled into the store and closed the door

behind him. "We had a ball at the game. My father really enjoyed having Tyson along. They hit it off immediately. It appears that they have another so called sport in common. Wrestling." His eyes danced with amusement at the mention of the fake sport that came on television.

Angela wanted to know more about the wedding that Tyson had mentioned.

Tyson slipped off his coat and tossed it on the counter. "Mom, Quinton's dad is getting married. He wants us to come to the wedding. Can we go? He told me there's going to be plenty of food and music and just good times. All of it is going to be Quinton's gift to his father and his new mom."

A flood of relief coursed through Angela. She grinned at Quinton. "That's right. I had forgotten all about your father and Miss Beatrice's ceremony. I saw their stunning engagement picture in the paper. It's right before Thanksgiving, isn't it?"

Quinton nodded and came to stand near Angela. "It's the weekend before Thanksgiving," he informed her. "My father said they had run out of invitations, but he wanted me to make sure that you and Tyson knew that he and his bride-to-be would love to have you share the day with them."

Tyson stood near his mother, waiting for her response. "So, can we make it, Mom?"

Angela saw the excitement on Tyson's face and knew there was no way she could refuse the invitation.

"I suppose we can go. I'm sure Christina can handle the store for one day. Maybe she can get one of her college friends to help her." She sneaked a look at Quinton, who was dashing, standing with his short leather jacket open and his hands jammed in his pocket.

"We'll be there. I can afford to miss one day at the store." Angela draped her arm around Tyson's shoulder and looked him in the eyes. "You do know you won't be able to wear your sneakers and jeans to this occasion?" She chuckled.

Tyson looked dismayed for a moment. "Yeah, I know. I can stand a necktie for a couple of hours to see Mr. Calvin get married."

Quinton said, " It only took one football game for them to become buddies. I'm going to have to watch this son of yours or else he'll take my place with my old man." He reached over and delivered a playful jab to Tyson's shoulder.

Laughing and backing away, Tyson held up his hands to block Quinton's action.

Amused, Angela clapped her hands to get their attention. "Boys, quit it now. I won't have any roughhousing in my store."

"Yes ma'am," Quinton answered her. "Oh, the wedding is next Saturday at five o'clock."

"That's short notice, but we'll be able to make it," Angela said. "You guys haven't told me anything about the game."

Tyson's brown eyes sparkled. "It was great. Our team won. Mr. Calvin is a lot fun, Mom, cheering for our boys."

"I'm glad you enjoyed yourself," she said to her son. She stared at Quinton. "Thanks for letting him tag along with you and your father."

"No problem," Quinton said. "He can hang out with us any time." He turned his attention to Tyson. "There's a big football game in December. I know you'll enjoy that as much as the one we attended today."

"We'll see about that," Angela said, giving her son a no nonsense glance. "I have to see how he does with his school assignments and how well he keeps his room in order."

"Mom," Tyson groaned. "I'm going to do all of that stuff." Then he looked at Quinton. "I'll be able to go. No sweat."

Quinton patted him on the back. "I hope you do. My dad and I don't want to miss your company. But we can always bring you souvenirs from the out-of-town game," he said in a teasing manner to Tyson.

"No, you won't, Uncle Que. I'll be there," Tyson said confidently.

Angela stood behind Tyson and placed her hands on his shoulder. "Fine, Tyson. Let's hope so. But right now, I need you to pick up in the storage room for me before we head for home. And it would be really nice if you ran the vacuum out here too."

Tyson glanced at her as though he wanted to protest, but didn't. He noticed how Quinton was staring at him. "I got it, I got it," he agreed. He lumbered away toward the back.

"Tyson, didn't you forget something?" Angela chided.

"Thanks, Uncle Que. See you, later," Tyson said, continuing to the back.

"You're welcome. See you, Tyson."

Angela looked at Quinton and shook her head. "He's something else. But I'm grateful for the change in his attitude and the fact that you've gotten through to him." She gave him a kind look.

"Tyson is a good kid. He just needed to be set straight about some things," he said, staring at her.

Angela shifted her eyes away from his. He'd awakened a part of her that she had thought had died. She turned away from him and stepped over to a nearby display that needed to be organized. "We've been quite busy," she informed him to draw attention away from herself.

"We got a new shipment of the latest novels in this week. Why don't you take a look? You might find something that Taylor likes."

At the mention of Taylor's name he gave her a peculiar look. Then he stepped up close to her and touched her ear.

Angela was taken by surprise by his move. She

reared away from him.

"Wait a minute. It's your earring. Let me hook it back before you lose it." He smiled at her and fastened her pierced hoop earring.

The simple touch of his hand rubbing her earlobe sent a delicious sensation through her. The fresh smell of his distinctive cologne tickled her nose and titillated her senses. It didn't take him long to make the adjustment. Once he moved away and turned his attention to the books she had been speaking of, she couldn't deny that she had been affected by the feel of his body close to hers. Her heart raced and her mind was clouded by a swirl of emotions that she knew she had no business feeling for him. Befuddled by all she felt, she stepped back so quickly that she knocked over a new display, sending the books tumbling to the floor. Flustered and embarrassed, she dropped to her knees to gather them up.

Looking amused, Quinton knelt to help her.

His assistance made her even more nervous. She lost her balance and fell backward on her bottom. She cursed silently. She hated him seeing her looking so clumsy. Chuckling to hide her embarrassment, she said, "It's time for me to go home and get some rest."

Quinton stood and bent over to extend a hand to help her up.

Embarrassed by her clumsiness, she took hold of it and allowed him to pull her to her feet. When he did, she fell upon his chest. He took hold of her shoulders and stared deeply into her eyes. In that instant, she noticed how his handsome face radiated a softness that transcended friendship. An emotional wave washed through her, filling her heart with a kind of tenderness that she recognized as desire. Looking in his warm, honey-col-ored-eyes, she dared to dream and to hope that romance could bloom within her heart. Holding his glance, she felt as though a spell had been cast on her. Quinton gave her a smile that was as intimate as a kiss. It accelerated her breathing; she licked her lips as though she could taste his sensual lips. Quinton let his hands slide up her arms and lowered his head as though he were about to kiss her.

The sudden roar of the vacuum cleaner was followed by the appearance of Tyson, shoving it as though he were mowing a lawn. Quinton and Angela jumped apart. They blinked and peered bashfully at each other as though they had been caught stealing.

Quinton wiped the bridge of his nose where beads of perspiration stood. "I've got to be going. I'm expected at the bar," he explained.

"Of course...yeah, sure," Angela stammered. "Uh, Tyson and I are going to finish in here and then be on our way. It's been...been a long day." She placed her hand over her heart even though she really wanted to use it to fan herself to cool down from the heat of passion he had stirred in her.

Quinton strolled toward door with Angela following

him. "Thanks again for taking Tyson," she said.

Wheeling, he faced Angela and gave her a longing look, as though he had something he wanted to say but couldn't find the words. He sighed. "Uh...make sure you lock the door behind me." He hesitated. "I can stay and wait..."

"No, go on. We'll be fine. My car is parked right outside the door. And the other stores are still open for another couple of hours. We'll be fine," she told him.

"I'll see you," he said in a quiet tone. He bestowed on her a wistful smile, then left.

The moment that he left, Angela returned to the clutter of books that remained on the floor. Picking up the books and arranging them where they should be placed, she couldn't help thinking of what had nearly happened between her and Quinton. Could it be that he was attracted to her? she mused. And she had been drawn to him like a magnet. If her son hadn't come through with the vacuum, the two of them could have done something that would have complicated the comfortable relationship they shared for the sake of Tyson. Angela eyed her son, who hustled with the vacuum around the store. It was obvious that he wanted to get the job done as quickly as he could. She was going to have to be more cautious around Quinton. The purpose of him coming around was for Tyson's benefit, not for the two of them to flirt as though they were college kids. Preoccupied, Angela went to the cash register to remove the money and place it the bank bag for its deposit. Just for a moment she dared to think of what Tyson's reaction might be if she were to get serious with Quinton. She knew he liked Quinton. But if she were romantically involved with him, would he come to resent him? He had come to think of himself as the man of the house. And his adolescent mind might not comprehend the fact that his mother needed companionship. The boy might be threatened by the fact of sharing his mother's affection with another man, she mused. Although things had gotten awful between Cole and her during the last few years of their marriage, they had kept their problems from Tyson. As far as Tyson knew, his father and mother had been a happy couple. Then after Cole was killed in the line of duty, Angela had seen no reason to bring up all the bad stuff that Cole had put her through. Cole had died a hero. And she wanted her son to go on believing good things about his father. She knew that thinking his father was anything less than perfect would devastate him. She had had enough problems with Tyson. She didn't want to mess his mind up by telling him things that his father wasn't around to defend or explain. She loved Tyson too much to let what was done and over damage him psychologically.

Lost in thought, she had been unaware that Tyson had completed the vacuuming. He eased up on her, causing her to jump.

"Mom, are you ready yet?" he asked, slipping his

coat on. "Wrestling is coming on television soon. I don't want to miss any of it."

Angela reached out and touched her son's face. The older he got, the more he looked like his father. She knew that the girls were going to be crazy for him the same way they had been for his father when he had been a college student.

Tyson smiled bashfully at her. "Mom, what's the matter? You've been acting weird since I got back from the game."

Angela grabbed the night deposit bag, slipping it inside her tote bag and grabbed her coat from the chair behind the counter. "I'm okay. I was just looking at you and wondering where my little boy went. You're growing up so fast."

Tyson stood tall and grinned. Then his eyes widened with excitement. "Hey, I almost forgot something. I need to get a copy of the latest *Jet.* Mr. Calvin was telling me that there's a picture of Quinton with Taylor Brown." He rushed over to the magazine rack and reached for a copy of the magazine and flipped the pages until he found the picture. He laughed. "Wow! Uncle Que got him a fine honey," he exclaimed, studying the picture.

"Does Quinton talk about Taylor much?" she asked, trying not to appear too interested.

Tyson flipped to the other pictures in the magazine. "Nope. It was his dad who did all the talking about her.

He told me he hasn't met her yet. Taylor lives in California and is on tour across the country with her new album. She might come and visit later on, I heard Quinton tell his dad." He placed the magazine back on the shelf and gave his mom an anxious look. "You ready yet, Mom?"

"Yes, I am. Let's get out of here." Angela gathered her things, turned out the lights and set the alarm. All the while she thought how foolish she had been to get caught up in that little flirtation with Quinton. He had that gorgeous, talented, younger Taylor Brown in his life. He wouldn't be interested in her, a stressed-out widow with a half-grown son.

Later that evening after Tyson had gone off to bed, Angela lay propped up in her bed reading the latest self-help book in hopes of mending her lonely spirit. However, she had only read a few paragraphs when she began to drift off to sleep envisioning Quinton's handsome face warmed by his beautiful smile...

Though Quinton's Corner had closed, Angela was relieved when she saw Quinton's car still on the parking lot. She was also grateful that it was the only one. Dressed in only a long red overcoat, she had come to declare her feelings for Quinton. She wanted him and tonight she had shown up at two a.m to make him aware that she was the kind of woman that he needed. Hopefully, what she had in mind would erase any thoughts, any emotions he had for Taylor Brown.

Getting out of her car, and wearing red high heels, she hurried up to the bar and knocked on the door to gain entrance. Quinton strolled from the back of his place where his office was located, wearing an annoyed expression. His face melted into a smile when he saw Angela. He unlocked the door to admit her into the darkened place. "What in the world are you doing out this time of morning?" he asked, holding open the door for her.

In the place that was dimly lit from the lights on the parking lot, Angela tilted her head and gave him a titillating smile. She ran her hand through her shiny raven hair and let her coat fall open to reveal the short black satin gown she wore. "I had trouble sleeping. I couldn't stop thinking about you and the way you made me feel in the store today. You wanted to kiss me and I wanted you to." She let the coat slide down over her shoulders and gave him a longing look.

Quinton scanned her critically and beamed with approval. He stepped up to her and placed his hand on the back of her neck, drawing her to him. "I've been thinking of you too, lovely one. What a treat to have you to show up this way." He crushed his mouth to hers; he shoved the coat away from her body. He fitted his hands at her back and ran them up and down her curvy body.

Angela wrapped her arms around his neck and pressed her body against his strong physique. The thin, satin fabric couldn't conceal the heat within her or him.

87

She parted her lips and welcomed his probing tongue. The intimacy of their kiss thrilled her to the core of her. She grew wet and moist, aching for him. She returned his kisses eagerly and began to sway her hips back and forth against his tantalizing manly bulge. Soon she felt him lift up her gown so that he could grip her bottom. Discovering she wore no lingerie, he groaned and held her tightly against him. He began to grind against her.

She grew limp in his arms and went with the warm sensation that consumed her. She lifted the sweater he wore and layered his chest with feathery hot kisses. He placed his knee in between her legs and rubbed it against her mound, teasing her with a sweet back and forth motion. She fell upon his chest and held on to his shoulder while she ground against him. She made a low, sizzling noise that let him know that she liked what he did.

Gripping her bottom, Quinton lifted her off the floor and carried her to a table in back. He set her there and lifted the gown over her head, flinging it to the floor. He unbuckled his pants, unzipped them and let them fall to floor along, with his boxers. Giving her a smoldering look, he parted her thighs and buried his ready arousal inside her. Once he was inside her, he encouraged her to wrap her legs around his waist. He leaned on her and proceeded to thrust with a steady tempo that made her feel as though she were glowing from head to toe. The sensation was heavenly and hypnotic. His arousal made her feel whole and complete. She pressed her thighs against his well-toned hips and relished the feel of love-making. To add to her heady emotions, Quinton fondled her breasts then nuzzled first one and then the other with wet, greedy kisses and suckled them until she felt as though she would faint with joy. Her breathing grew loud and labored; she locked her legs tighter around his body, urging him on. Soon, Quinton moved faster and harder inside her. As their bodies whipped against each other, she called out his name and surrendered her all to him as she reached an explosive climax that caused her to tremble and him to quiver and groan as though he were drowning from the pleasures of her body...

"Mom! Mom!" called Tyson, standing over his mother and shaking her awake.

Angela stared up at her son as though she didn't recognize him. As the fog of her dream passed, she bolted upright in bed. "Tyson, what...what's wrong?" She wiped perspiration from her brow then laid her hand on her chest where her heart raced from the erotic dream.

"From my room I could hear you moaning. Are you okay? Were you having a nightmare?" he asked, looking concerned.

Angela's face burned with guilt over the dream she'd had. "No, baby. I'm fine. I...I was having a nightmare. But...I'm fine. You go on back to bed." She reached up and hugged her son before she urged him on.

Once Tyson had returned to his room, Angela fell back on her bed. Her body burned from the vivid inter-

Sinclair LeBeau

lude in the fantasy she had shared with Quinton. In her mind she had reasoned that a relationship with Quinton was out of the question. It just wasn't practical. Yet her body and heart were betraying her. She sighed and lay awake, wishing that the dream could be a reality.

Chapter 5

During conversation at breakfast, Angela scowled at her son with his latest disclosure of a school assignment. "When did the teacher make this assignment, Tyson?" Her lips thinned in irritation.

During breakfast, Tyson sat sprawled in the kitchen chair across from her. "The teacher made the assignment three weeks ago. I sort of forgot," he mumbled.

Angela folded her arms, feeling frustrated. "If I had known about this assignment, I certainly wouldn't have allowed you to attend that wrestling match at the arena this past Saturday with Quinton and his father. You could have used that time to work on this project," she fumed, hearing about the work that her son had due the next day. There was no way she could manage to help him. Her day, her evening would be busy. All of Our Best had been chosen to provide the books for a lecture and book signing by a popular author for one of the most prestigious Black business ladies' organizations in the area. The event was being held at a banquet hall in a hotel downtown. This was the evening that Angela was going to have a chance to shine as a professional and to promote her store with other career-minded women. The last thing she needed today was to be bogged down by yet another thoughtless act of her teen son.

"Tyson, what am I going to do with you? How can I get you to be responsible?" She eyed her son, feeling helpless. "I don't know what I can do to help you now. I have an obligation this evening that I can't afford to cancel. I can't be like you and do what I want when I get ready to." Her voice quivered with emotions of frustration and anger.

Blinking nervously at his mother's response, Tyson sat upright in his chair. "Mom, maybe I can get Uncle Que to help me. He always tells me to call him whenever I have a problem or need him."

"Tyson, your Uncle Que has a business and he's a busy man," Angela said. She sipped on her coffee, furrowing her brow with worry. "Yes, he said you could call him, but it doesn't mean you're to impose on him unnecessarily."

Ignoring his mother's words, Tyson jumped from his chair and rushed to the telephone. "I'm going to call him.

He'll help me," he said with confidence.

Angela pursed her lips and pretended not to care what her son did. Secretly, though, she hoped that Quinton would come through for Tyson. She hated the idea of his failing. It was the last thing he needed. She grabbed the morning paper and opened it as she eavesdropped on her son's conversation.

"Yo Uncle Que, you still sleep?" Tyson spoke loudly into the receiver.

Eyeing her kitchen clock, she noticed that it was six forty-five. And she assumed that Quinton had probably been sound asleep until the phone call. She knew he pulled late hours at his bar. Amused, she could just imagine Quinton, wondering if Tyson had lost his mind by waking him up so early. Right about now, she bet that Quinton was having second thoughts about this mentoring business. Quinton had no idea how crazy a thirteen-year-old could make you.

"Science project. It's due tomorrow. I need a poster that has something to do with the body.   Stuff like the heart, lungs and..." He paused, listening. "My mother has an important meeting to go to this evening, so she can't help me," Tyson explained and glanced over his shoulder at his mother who acted as though she were absorbed in the newspaper. "Yeah, she's kind of pissed. I kind of forgot the assignment." He paused again. "I didn't tell her until this morning.. Will you help me? Please," Tyson implored Quinton as though he were a little angel.

Still eavesdropping on the conversation, Angela moved out of her chair and began clearing their breakfast dishes.

"Gee, thanks Uncle Que," Tyson enthused. He glanced at his mother and gave her a thumbs up sign. "Yeah, I need some stuff to make it with. I get out of school at two-twenty. You'll pick me up and take me to get what I need? You're all right!" he said. "See ya, man."

He hung up the phone and wheeled around on his sneakers, grinning from ear to ear. "Mom, Uncle Que can help me. He has a friend who teaches biology. He's going to give him a call and get everything I need from this guy. He says he'll get his friend to give us a good topic that won't take up a lot of time. Quinton's going to pick me up from school and take me get everything we'll need for the project." Tyson sighed. "Uncle Que told me I might not get an "A," but he's sure that we'll be able to get something together, so I won't get a failing grade."

Though Angela was relieved, she kept a blank expression. "I'm glad that he could help you this time. But, Tyson, I want you to be more responsible. What were you going to do if you couldn't have called him, boy?"

Tyson just shrugged and strolled to the counter where his backpack lay. "It won't happen again. I promise, Mom." He gave her a smile that reminded her of his father's charm. She knew that it was her son's attempt at sweetening her annoyance with him. "Uncle Que is bringing me home to work on the project. He told me he'll fill me in then on whatever his friend comes up with. It'll probably take all evening, but it's going to be fun working with him. Just wait until the guys see him pick me up from school. They're going to be too psyched." His eyes danced with glee.

Cupping his chin in her hand, Angela stared at him and pointed her finger. "Don't let this happen again. You keep up with your work. Understand."

Tyson nodded. "I will. I will," he said, wiggling away from her. "I've got to go or else I'll miss the school bus and you'll have to take me."

"Get out of here," she ordered in a playful tone. "I have too much to do to play chauffeur to you today."

Tyson bounded toward the door, "Bye, Mom," he called right before he slammed the door behind himself.

🌹 🌹 🌹

It was nearly eleven o'clock when Angela came home from the book event. The night had been an emotional roller coaster. The author of a touching and heartbreaking coming-of-age memoir of a young black girl growing up in poverty in the South was the speaker. Her reading from her book was a passage telling of the obstacles she overcame to become a successful cardiologist at one of the top medical hospitals in the country. It had been inspirational. Everything had gone well until Angela got ready to set out the author's books to sell and be signed. Assuming that Christina could be trusted with the chore of setting out the right boxes, Angela hadn't bothered to check them until the speaker was nearly done. It was then that she discovered that the wrong books had been brought to the banquet hall by Christina's lovesick boyfriend who had offered to help them. The evening was nearly disastrous. Angela felt as though her credibility had been ruined by the mix-up. Her breathing had grown short and she had broken out in a sweat, symptoms of a classic panic attack. There had been about a hundred women at the event who were anxious to buy books to be signed. Thankfully the physician/author was a gracious person. When humiliated Angela explained the dilemma, the kind author suggested to Angela that she could make a list of the people who wanted to buy her book. She would gladly come to her store the following morning and autograph the books. Then Angela could deliver the books or have the customers pick them up at her store. Angela agreed and made the announcement, thinking that the women wouldn't go along with the idea. But surprisingly, they agreed with the solution. Despite the blunder, Angela was pleased to realize at the evening's end that she had sold nearly all of the books that were sitting in her stockroom at the store. And many of the women who hadn't been to her store were more than interested in coming to All of Our Best to pick up their books, so that they could see the new business run by the attractive, young woman.

Reaching her home and pulling into her driveway, she was comforted by the sight of Quinton's jeep. She had been so preoccupied by her problems that she hadn't worried about Tyson and the assignment he had due. She hoped that Quinton had been able to help Tyson pull together the science project that was due the next day.

Entering the house, she slipped out of her high heels and pulled off the jacket to the gray suit she had worn. She tugged her deep blue blouse out of her skirt and went to the dining room where she heard Tyson and Quinton talking.

Tyson glanced up at his drowsy-looking mother. "We just finished,"he announced, turning the poster board for her to view. "Isn't it great? We did it on the circulatory system."

Angela stared at the board and was impressed by the neat diagram of the inner workings of the body. It was bright and colorful and full of information. "Good job, guys," she said, smiling at Tyson. She beamed at Quinton with appreciation. "I'm glad that you were able to help him pull this together. Tyson and I are going to have to treat you to dinner or something for taking your valuable time the way you did."

Quinton rubbed the side of his face and stared at Angela. "Hmm...I'll take some of your home cooking.

If I remember correctly, you could make a meat loaf that was out of this world. I don't get a chance to get much soul cooking like that."

Standing behind Tyson, she touched the sides of the boy's smooth face. "My fabulous meatloaf will be yours. Just let me know when you have the time to come to dinner." Her hands slid down to her son's shoulders to urge him out of his seat. "You need to get to bed, mister," she ordered.

Yawning, Tyson got out of his seat and started to clear away the clutter from the project.

"Leave that," Angela insisted. "I'll get that myself," she said, waving him to go off toward his bedroom.

Tyson leaned against his mother and hugged her around her waist. "Thanks Uncle Que. Good-night, Mom. I'll let you know what grade *we* made," he chuckled, looking at Quinton, then began to saunter away.

"You're welcome, man. I enjoyed the work. I forgot how much fun learning could be," Quinton said, sitting at the dining room table looking a bit worn from the long session he'd had with Tyson.

Tyson froze and turned to scowl at Quinton. "Fun?" Then he disappeared to his room.

Quinton shook his head. "Kids just don't know what a good deal they have. I only wish I could go back to where he is. How about you?"

Angela grew thoughtful. "I sure would. There would be so many things I would do differently. So

98

many more things I would take advantage of."

"Yeah, I know what you mean," Quinton said.

Angela began to clear away the colored markers, the reference books and the excess construction paper that the two of them had used.

Jumping to his feet, Quinton proceeded to help Angela. "How was your event?" He eyed her, noticing how tired she looked. He was also aroused by her appearance. She looked as though she needed to be hugged and showed special attention by a caring man like himself.

"Oh my goodness, it started out terrible. But things worked out for the better," she said, taking handfuls of excess paper and tossing them into the nearby waste basket. "Christina had her boyfriend deliver the wrong boxes. But I guess when you're as in love as those two kids are your mind stays clouded. I can't wait to see her and let her know how her romance nearly ruined me."

Quinton studied her face and grinned. "Ah, young love. There's nothing like it."

"I guess I can't be too hard on them. I do remember what it's like to be head-over-heels in love. It's a beautiful feeling. Too bad that it can't be bottled and sadder still that it doesn't last." Stacking the books on the end of the table, she stared at Quinton. "Come on into the kitchen and let me prepare you a snack I'm starving. I haven't eaten much all day. I was too nervous about pulling this thing off." She turned away from him and stepped in the direction of the kitchen.

Quinton took hold of her arm. "Uh, Angela, Tyson and I kind of left the kitchen in a mess. He and I ordered a pizza and then we sort of cleaned out the other goodies you had in there while we were working. But I'm going to clean it all up. I'll have it gleaming in a matter of moments." He stepped in front of her and entered the kitchen, pushing up his sleeves.

Angela followed him and saw that he hadn't exaggerated. She glanced at the mess on the kitchen table. There were two pizza boxes, empty soda cans, open bags of chips and cookies, and crumbs all over the counter. There were several glasses with the remains of watered-down soda and juice in them. She stared at Quinton and shook her head, amused. "How in the world did you two find time to work?"

Quinton shrugged. "That boy of yours has quite an appetite. And every time he ate, I ate too. I can't hang out with him too much or else I'm going to find myself out of shape." He chuckled and set to clearing away the clutter.

While he cleaned, she went to the refrigerator and searched for something tasty.

"I saw some deli ham and cheese in there," Quinton informed her. "Why don't you have a seat and let me serve you? You look as though you could use the pampering." He went to her, placed his hands on her shoulders and steered her away from the fridge to a stool at her

100

kitchen counter.

Angela didn't put up a fight. She liked the idea of coming home and finding an adult she could share her troubles with, not to mention one who had been able to reach her son. Watching Quinton while he prepared her sandwich, she admired his stance and the evident strength in his physique. His sweater and jeans showed off the bulk in his arms and revealed the shape of his tight bottom and well-toned thighs. Angela felt a flush of warmth on the back of her neck. She was assessing him as though she were sizing him up to seduce him. Carnal pleasure with him would be delightful, she imagined. Her body yearned to be satisfied by a man who wanted her in every way. At this point in her life, was there such a man like that for her? she wondered remorsefully. Her marriage bed had been cold for several years before Cole's death. Cruelly, he had shut down the physical side of their marriage. His action had hurt her and made her feel less than a woman. But now, watching the graceful way that Quinton moved around her kitchen, her repressed sexual feelings surfaced. She had loved sex with Cole. He had been her first and only lover. As long as she had believed that he loved her as much as she loved him, there was nothing better than being in bed and caught up in the thrills of being a woman.

Quinton broke into Angela's thoughts with a grand gesture of setting a plate of food and glass of iced cola before her. "For the hard-working lady. Enjoy." He smiled at her.

The sandwich looked delicious. "I could get used to this," she said before picking up the food and taking a bite. "I'm not used to being pampered."

Quinton, who had a can of soda, leaned on the counter near Angela, sipping on it. "Is it okay if I turn on the radio?" he asked, reaching in front of her to turn on the radio sitting on the table near her. When he did, his arm accidentally brushed against her breast.

A tingling sensation shot through her and she could feel her nipple tightening. "That's fine. Music always soothes me."

Music from one of those "Quiet Storm" programs filled the room. The song reminded Angela of her short-lived college career and the fall she had met Cole and been taken in by his charms. She didn't want to go back to that time. It had all been a dream that turned into a nightmare with the exception of their son. She reached over and switched the station to a jazz station.

"Hey, I was grooving on that song," Quinton protested.

"I wasn't. Too many memories," she admitted. She had eaten only half of her sandwich before pushing it aside.

Quinton recognized her distress and gave her a sympathetic look. "Certain songs hit me that way too. Some of them can transport you to a time when your life was simple, fun. Then there are those that only remind you of things you'd rather forget. Some of those songs can reach down in you and open up wounds that you had convinced yourself were healed." Quinton stared at her, conveying his understanding.

"You've hit it right on the head. That song took me back to when we were in college. It was my first semester at Riley U. I was young and naive and bitten by the charms of Cole Etheridge. I remember seeing him and thinking what an angel of a man he was. He was the most gorgeous, sexy guy I'd ever met. Every girl on campus had a crush on him. Yet, he had singled me out. I was literally swept off my feet by his magnetism. Although I had come to college for an education, I also wanted to fall in love. I knew that I would meet my husband by the time I graduated from college. Of course, I had imagined that my campus dream man and I would share one of these idyllic romantic relationships while we were in college and that by the time I was a graduating senior, he and I would be making plans to have a romantic wedding in the campus chapel." Her voice was dreamy and full of the hope she had once had. "Unfortunately, it was far from idyllic. I ended up getting pregnant. I was happy that Cole wanted to do the right thing by marrying me. And I believed that our marriage would work because of the baby we had made. However, at nineteen I had no idea that a baby has no way of making someone love you. I tried to convince myself in those days that I meant more to Cole that just some silly freshman virgin he had bagged. You know the deal, Quinton."

Quinton took a seat on the stool beside Angela and faced her. "Cole cared for you," he said to comfort her. "He respected you and..."

"Yeah, yeah. But he wasn't in love with me. He and I had decided to divorce right before he was killed."

Quinton reached over and touched her on the arm. "That was unfortunate. Cole had a lot of issues in his life. If it's any comfort to you, I don't believe he was capable of giving love to anyone other than Tyson. Leaving you, he would have only gone from woman to woman. True, he was my good friend and I knew I could count on him when I had problems. However, he had difficulty dealing with his feelings for women. I'm not a psychologist and I don't know where his insecurity with women came from."

Angela patted Quinton's hand and moved away from him. "Tyson is unaware of what went on between his father and me. I want him to hold on to that image of Cole as being a perfect father and husband. What good would it do, Quinton, to tell him otherwise?" Angela went to the stove and got the teakettle to fill with water for a soothing cup of tea.

"I have to admire you for that. Tyson thinks the world of his old man. In the last few weeks that I've been with him, he has told me how Cole used to make him promise to look after the house and to take care of you whenever he would have to go off for days on duty at the fire station."

Angela leaned against the sink with her arms folded at her waist. She smiled sadly. "Tyson likes to think that he is capable of looking after me and protecting me. Bless his little heart."

Quinton stood and strolled toward Angela. "Cole has been gone going on three years now. Have you considered dating or the possibility of marrying again?"

She was momentarily rendered speechless by this personal question. "I...well, no. After Cole was killed, I felt as though I had been put through the wringer, emotionally. At the time of his death, I was dealing with my anger and pain over our decision to divorce. Then there was his death that took me into another emotional dimension. I had to consider my son and put up a front for him to help him get through his grief."

"But it's your time now. You're still a young woman. I certainly hope you don't intend to live your life alone. Tyson is half grown. And he has his mind on the young ladies. Your baby is growing up." He looked amused.

"Tyson has talked to you about girls," she said, taken by surprise. She'd thought this wouldn't be an issue for another couple of years.

Quinton nodded. "He likes a girl in his science class. He has to make an oral presentation on what we did tonight. He wanted me to tell him what to wear because he's nervous about standing in front the class and worrying about the kind of impression he's going to make on this girl named Mia."

Angela placed her hands up to her face and shook her head, looking concerned. "I'm not ready for this."

"You're going to have to get used to it. He and I have talked man-to-man about some things that I know would make you blush. He's at the age where he needs to know things about sex, birth control and sexual diseases. I hope you don't mind. The boy is curious." Quinton stared at her, hoping she wouldn't resent the frank conversations he had with Tyson.

"Oh no," she said, feeling grateful. "I'm glad that he has you to talk with. I believe there are things that only a man can tell a growing boy." Angela stood staring in space. She thought of Tyson and his interest in sex and girls. The next few years were going to be full of many challenges. She wondered if she was going to be able to keep her son on the right track. She had to make sure that he wouldn't make the same mistake she had when she was young. And she certainly hoped he wouldn't grow into the kind of man his father was who used woman only as sexual objects. Thinking back over her past, she realized she had become sexually active before she was ready emotionally. No doubt sex with the right person and when you thought you were in love could be the most beautiful experience of your life. That first flame of love and the first time making love were magical. But there were also consequences and complications that could result from sweet pleasure shared in the heat of passion.

The teakettle whistled loudly. Angela rushed to remove the pot from the burner. "Would you like some tea, coffee or hot chocolate?" she asked Quinton.

"No thanks," he said, glancing at his watch. "It's getting late. I need to run by the Corner and check on things." He gave her a polite smile and turned to leave.

"Well, thanks again for everything," she said, following him into the living room where he had tossed his leather jacket. She watched him slip into it, observing the way his gray turtleneck sweater fitted across his broad chest and was tucked down into his jeans, showing off his trim waist and flat abdomen. Suddenly she was hit with loneliness. After the day she'd had, she wished that she had a man like Quinton to love and to enfold her in his arms, calming all of her insecurities about raising her teen son on her own.

Quinton noticed her sad, reflective expression. He placed his hand under her chin and looked into her eyes. "Hey, what's going on in that pretty head of yours? Is there anything you want to talk about? I can stay so we can talk," he offered.

A shiver went through her from his simple action. She met his smoldering, wonderful eyes framed by his handsome square face and wished that she had the nerve to reveal what her needs were. "I...I'm okay. It's just that when I've had a particularly rough day things are a bit overwhelming. And...and sometimes I wish I had someone I could lean on...to comfort me." Feeling vulnerable, she couldn't look at him. She turned her head and stepped back as though she didn't trust what she might do next.

Quinton placed his hands on her arms. "Not only am I here for Tyson, but I want you to feel that you can talk to me as well. As long as I'm around, you don't have to feel that you're all on your own." His voice was soothing. The sound of his voice alerted her feminine sensibilities and she was touched by the tenderness she saw in his eyes. She yearned to have him wrap his arms around her and hold her against him. She craved the physical nearness of a man, but was too proud to admit her need. Despite the smile she wore each day, no one could imagine how lonely and how inadequate Cole had left her. Before their decision to divorce and then his death, he had done a good job of making her doubt herself as a woman who was capable of attracting any man.

"It's kind of you to say that," she said, finally finding her voice. "But you have a life. I can't keep running to you with all of my problems. The things going on with me I will work out. I'm not completely helpless."

He gave her an amiable, musing look. "Okay, superwoman. It's been great being able to see you and Tyson again. There's nothing that gives me more pleasure than being with him these days. Seeing him comforts me; I see so much of Cole in him. You can't imagine how much I miss Cole. I know he was far from perfect, but he was my friend. There was a lot of good in him, and I see those good qualities in Tyson. That, along with your sweetness, is going to turn Tyson into a wonderful man."

Angela laughed gently and rested her hands on his arms. "I certainly hope so." Realizing she had gotten too comfortable with him, she released his arms and turned away toward the door to open it for him. Suddenly he took hold of her arm and pulled her back to him and against him. He kissed her. Stunned by his action, Angela's body went rigid. But the feel of his lips melded against hers sent spirals of desire through her. The kiss that had started out as a tender one turned into one full of hungry passion. It enflamed her and drugged her senses. The feel of his strong arms locked around her was like a balm to her wounded spirit. She responded to his warmth by wrapping her arms around his neck and pressing her body against his. She grew dizzy with her lust and hunger for a man. Quinton's lips wandered to the side of her face and down her neck, searing her flesh. When Quinton started to unbutton her blouse, she seized his hand. With her heart racing, she exhaled deeply to clear her head. She looked at him. "What are we doing?" She stepped away from him, feeling betrayed by her body. Her core had grown moist and her nipples ached for the feel of his wet, hot lips there.

There was a longing look in his eyes. "I...I wanted to make you feel better. I only meant to give you a friendly kiss of comfort. Tasting your honey-flavored lips, I got carried away," he said in an apologetic tone. "You want this too. I could tell by the way you held me, kissed me. It's all right."

He moved closer to her; he lifted her skirt and placed a knee between hers. He palmed the side of her face and nibbled on her lips before parting them with his tongue. Once again, Angela surrendered to his touch. She closed her eyes and allowed herself to be transported to a paradise where she had been a stranger for far too long. Quinton's knee rested deliciously on her feminine mound. He brushed it back and forth in a rhythmic tempo that was akin to lovemaking. And she loved the way the action invigorated her. She fell forward and clung to his broad shoulders while she swirled her hips to intensify the pleasure she felt between her legs.

Quinton gripped her bottom and kissed her harder still. He removed his knee and held her against his bulging manhood. He pressed himself against her, moaning and breathing hotly.

Soon, her center burst from the hot sensations that Quinton had elicited in her. As cascades of pleasure washed through her, she hugged him tightly and smothered her groans of delight in his chest. Spent physically and out of the hypnotic state of the erotic moment, she was suddenly flooded with shame. How could she have lost control the way she had with Quinton? What must he think of her, making out with him and grinding as though she had lost her mind and had no respect for herself? And most importantly, what if her teenage son had walked up on them and caught his mother with her skirt up around her waist doing it? Angela mused, tugging down her skirt and turning away from Quinton.

Quinton eased up behind her and placed his hands on her shoulders. "There's nothing to be ashamed about, Angela. I enjoyed every moment of it. You're a beautiful and passionate woman," he said in a gentle tone.

Tears of shame stung her eyes. She wouldn't turn to look at him. "You'd better go, Quinton. I don't want to talk about what happened," she said in a voice that was full of feelings of disgrace. She marched away from Quinton, leaving him to let himself out of the house.

Outside in the night air, Quinton's body still yearned for Angela. Though she had experienced release, he hadn't. But he had loved the way she looked and felt reaching her climax. If only he had had the chance to take her to bed and lay her out nude where he could kiss and touch every inch of her exquisite almond-colored flesh, he imagined that the intimacy would have been hot and deeply satisfying for them both. Just before he got in his car, he looked back at Angela's house and noticed the light on in her bedroom. He stared at the window and wondered if she had undressed and was nude. Just for a brief moment, he considered returning to the house and begging her to let him spend the night and share her bed. He was full of pent-up energy and passion that he want-

ed to expend with her only. The thought further aroused
him and made his manliness firm. He took a deep breath
and climbed into the car. He knew that he would have a
long, restless night ahead of him. He would toss and turn
the whole night through, remembering her sweet moan
and the feel of her body quivering against him in the
hallway.

Chapter 6

The next day Angela went to her store chagrined by her behavior with Quinton the night before. She couldn't believe how one kiss that she should have never accepted turned her on so completely, transforming her into a vixen. Quinton had responded in the way any man would with a woman who had been so openly wanton. Then she contemplated how far she had gone with him. His simple touch had rendered her irrational and weak. Despite her shameful response, she had to admit those moments of surrender had been marvelous. He reminded her of how good it was to be a woman. Quinton was a perfect specimen of a man; he had been sensitive and kind to her. He was the epitome of everything that she had needed and been missing in her life. She sighed, thinking how fresh and clean he smelled. The light citrus aroma of his cologne titillated her and sparked desire within her. And lately, whenever she looked into his marvelous eyes, she felt as though she were being placed under some kind of spell. The more she saw him the more intensely aware she became of the sensual, manly way he moved his body. If she didn't get a grip on herself, she feared that the sensuality and charisma that Quinton radiated could be lethal to her emotionally. During her marriage and when he had just been Quinton, Cole's friend, she hadn't been in tune to these magnetic qualities. But since he had re-entered her life as a mature man who knew who he was and had some ambition other than partying and trying to be with all the glamorous women he could, Angela had been intrigued by him. Like Tyson, she found herself looking forward to his visits. Thinking of the intimacy she had shared with Quinton, she wondered if they could go back to being just friends. In her heart, she was ready to explore a relationship. But she had Tyson to consider. Right now, he had to come first. She didn't want her son to feel confused or betrayed by a romance that probably didn't stand a chance. And there was no way she could compete with Taylor Brown who had some sort of place in his life.

Angela was grateful that she worked alone in the mornings during the week. Business had been slow with the exception of a few young housewives or senior citizens who dropped in to browse or to make a special purchase. She had plenty of stock to set out, but all she could do was sit and stare, thinking of the night before. One moment she was embarrassed by her actions and the next minute her body tingled thinking of how cozy and right she felt with Quinton.

Feeling kind of low and guilty from her actions, she had trouble concentrating. As hard she tried, she couldn't stop thinking of how delicious she'd felt in Quinton's arms. And then the next moment she would chide herself for her behavior. Angela was unnerved when she glanced up to see Quinton strolling into the store. Had she conjured him up by thinking of him constantly? She wasn't ready to face him yet. To make matters worse for her, he showed up looking debonair in shades and a designer sweater and slacks that matched perfectly. She hopped off the stool she had been perched on and grabbed an armful of books to look busier than she had been since she had arrived. She wanted to be moving around, so that Quinton couldn't enchant her the way he had the night before. No one was in the store for the moment and she didn't want to take the risk of her body betraying her again.

Smiling politely, Angela asked in a cheery tone, "Quinton, what are you doing out this way so early? You told me you were a late sleeper." Her heart thumped hard against her chest as she walked to a shelf and carefully placed the books in the proper places.

Quinton strode to her and reached over her shoulder to get a novel she had just placed on the shelf. "I usually do. But last night after I left you, I had trouble sleeping." He clutched the book to him and stared at her with a mischievous grin.

At the mention of the erotic episode, Angela turned to look at him. Her almond-colored complexion flooded with color. "Yes, you are the reason for my lack of sleep. You gave me quite a bit to think about." He stared at her warmly.

"Uh...I have been thinking about that too. I'm embarrassed, Quinton. I don't know what I could have been thinking. I'm usually so in control." She floundered under the intensity of his scrutiny.

Quinton's brow creased with concern. "There's nothing to be ashamed of. I happen to like whatever came over us and brought us together that way." A smile played at the corners of his mouth. "I liked being there with you when you were totally out of control."

Angela returned his smile with a blank expression. "I bet you got a kick out of getting next to me. I bet it pleases you to see that I'm just like all the other women who want to get next to the great Quinton Gibbs," she fumed. Her humiliation was so deep that she wanted to cry. "Is that why you came here today? To remind me that I'm no better than all the rest of your groupies?"

Quinton stared at her, baffled. She was acting as though it was the worst thing she could have done.

At that moment, a delivery man rushed through the door, carrying two loads of magazines. He plopped them in front of her newsstand and marched up to her. "How you doing, Mrs. Etheridge?" asked the tall, lanky man. He held out a clipboard for her to sign. He looked at Quinton and his eyes lighted with recognition. "Hey, you're that basketball player, 'Sweet Que.'"

Quinton extended his hand and gave the man a smile. "Yeah, that's me, brother."

The man grinned and shook his hand enthusiastically. "I sure miss seeing you play. The game is not the same without you, man. Too bad you had to retire because of a busted knee. Wait until I tell the family I met you." He beamed at Quinton with admiration.

Angela scribbled her name on the required form and handed it back to the man. "Thanks, Jeff," she responded to the guy.

The delivery man took the clipboard without looking at Angela. He reached into his shirt pocket and pulled out a note pad. "Could I get your autograph? My son would get a big kick out of it."

"Sure thing," Quinton said, obliging him by scrawling his name quickly on the pad and handing it back to him.

"Thank you, thank you," enthused the delivery man, backing out the door and staring at Quinton. "See you in two weeks, Mrs. Etheridge," he called as an after-thought as he finally disappeared through the door.

Once the delivery man had left, Quinton watched Angela kneeling on the floor and cutting away the strings on the bundled magazines. He could sense that his pres-ence wasn't welcome and that she wasn't interested in discussing the events of the past evening. Determined not to leave until he could find a way to get her to open up to him, he patiently watched her going through the various issues of magazines she had received. All the while, he tried to think of a way to express himself and to let her know that last night had meaning for him, that he hadn't meant for her to feel as though he were taking advantage of her. Then he noticed that among her mag-azines there was the latest issue of *Essence* with a gor-geous picture of Taylor Brown on the cover. He had been with Taylor during that photo session. The photographer was a friend of his and had done some shots of him for other publications. The timing for this was bad for him, especially now that he had an interest in Angela, he thought. He watched Angela study the picture with a blank expression. Rising from her knees, she handed him one of the copies she held. "Here's something of interest for you. A nice picture of your little girlfriend," she said. Then she read the blurb on the cover, "Taylor Brown talks about fame and her new romance." She raised an eyebrow in a questioning slant. "That new romance would be you, I'll bet. You may have the magazine compliments of All of Our Best. I'll bet you can't wait to read what your woman thinks of you." She turned away from him and busied herself carefully stocking her newsstand.

Quinton accepted the magazine and folded it and stuck it under his arm as though it didn't matter. "Taylor and I are not as close you think. Sure, I've taken her out a couple of times. But...well, there's nothing serious happening between us. She gets a lot of press when we're seen together," he explained. "To be honest, it's no fun being out with her. Everywhere we go we are followed by photographers, her fans, my fans and it's a big mess with everyone gawking at us." Without looking at him, she said in a sarcastic tone, "What a life. Really, Quinton. You don't owe me any explanations. Just because you and I messed around in my hallway doesn't make me your girlfriend." She chuckled. "Your personal life is your business. I certainly have too much going on in my own to concern myself with your life of glitz and glamour."

He grew irritated by her assumptions and her aloofness. Moving closer, he tried to get her attention. "Angela, don't dismiss last night," he persisted. "I want you to know that I do find you attractive. I know that I've always been considered only a family friend, but I'd like for you to think of me as more than just that." His silky voice held a challenge.

She found his words vaguely disturbing. Deep inside of her, she wanted to yield to his offer of affection. She stared at the magazine with Taylor's vivacious, alluring pose. She thought of the many pictures she had seen of the two of them lately in other magazines and the gossip she had read concerning their close relationship. Like Cole, Quinton once had been known for being quite a ladies' man. She had vowed to guard her heart and not to get hurt again. She had experienced too much heartache, too much loneliness and much too much anxiety over sharing her husband with other women. And Cole hadn't been the high profile personality that Quinton was. If she yielded to Quinton's charms, she would be a glutton for punishment, she reasoned. Taylor, the fabulous singer and sexy beauty, was better suited to his rich and famous lifestyle. She reached for one of the *Essence* magazines and displayed Taylor Brown's picture. "No thank you. I think you'd be happier with her."

Before Quinton could respond, a woman entered the store and began to browse.

Angela turned away from Quinton, trying to dismiss him and hoping he would leave. "Hello, can I help you find anything in particular?" she said in a much too cheery voice.

When the customer told Angela she wanted to browse, Angela returned to the counter and fumbled with the clutter there. Quinton followed her, feeling foolish for laying his emotions out for her to stomp on. He stood before her, rolling the magazine in his hands. "Angela, Taylor is a friend. She and I have dated. Nothing more. She dates other guys and I see whom I choose when I want." He stared at her. "I'd like to date you to get to know you as more than Tyson's mother or Cole's wife. Don't tell me you're afraid to have a simple date with me?" he challenged. "Not to be disrespectful or any-thing, but from your response last night I think you're more than ready to find someone to date, even if I'm not the lucky one." He grinned, his eyes filled with amuse-ment.

She glared at Quinton. But she couldn't defend her-self. She had shown him her vulnerability. "No, I think not. It might be too much for Tyson. He's had enough problems. Right now you seem to be doing a good job of getting through to him. If you and I were to begin dat-ing that might mess things up for him. And besides, I don't believe he's ready for me to date."

Quinton frowned. "Just who is the parent?"

Angela shot him an annoyed look. "I'm the parent. But I haven't discussed dating with my son. In his thirteen-year-old mind, he thinks that I shouldn't want or need another man. To him, no other man should take his father's place in my life or our home. Tyson feels that it's me and him against the world since his father's death."

Looking concerned, Quinton said, "But you're a young woman, Angela. There's going to come a time when you're going to want a life for yourself. And Tyson will be grown soon himself. He won't need you. You have to make him understand that you have to have a life. You have to let him know that you can still be his mother even though you may choose to have a relationship."

His words grated on her nerves. "Listen, I don't need you to tell me how to raise my son. I think I've done a pretty good job with him; that is, until now. I mean, I appreciate you mentoring him, but our family life is personal. What's between Tyson and me is of no concern to you."

The lone customer moved up to the counter and excused herself for interrupting the conversation.

Angela turned on her professional charm. "Ready to check out? Did you find everything you want?" she asked the woman.

Quinton stepped away from the counter and glanced

at the titles on the nearest shelf. Once the woman was gone, he turned back to Angela. "I hope you still have plans to attend my father's wedding."

After the situation last night, Angela had considered not going as a means of distancing herself from Quinton. But she knew how much Tyson was looking forward to attending the wedding and being with the Gibbs family on that day. She didn't want to back out.

"Tyson and I will be at the wedding," she said, scooping up some books from behind the counter and proceeding to move around the store to place and arrange them.

A look of relief flooded his face. "I'm glad to hear that," he said. "Uh...my father would be disappointed if Tyson didn't come. He's taken quite a liking to him. And then my father would also like to see you as well."

She smiled. "We'll be there," she said in a soft voice.

The store remained empty and Angela didn't bother to say anything more to Quinton. She didn't want to address the issue of their dating. As far as she was concerned, that was out of the question.

Then several people entered All of Our Best and wandered around the store, browsing. A young man approached Angela to request a special order of a book he needed.

While Angela went to her computer to work with her

customer, Quinton walked up to her and touched her on the arm. "I'm leaving. I'll be in touch," he said, smiling while he spoke.

Angela's heart turned over with the kindness she saw on Quinton's face. She nodded and continued working at the computer to assist her customer. However, she stole a glance at Quinton as he strolled out of the store. And for a moment, she wished she had the courage to date him. She had been flattered that he found her interesting. But there was the situation with Tyson.

How would he feel, seeing her date the man whom he had known as his father's friend? What would he think of her? she wondered. She sighed with resignation and dismissed the thought, refocusing attention on dealing with her customer. She couldn't get involved with Quinton Gibbs, she reasoned. She was better off placing all her energies into raising her son and running her bookstore. That was all she was capable of dealing with for right now.

Chapter 7

The wedding of Quinton's father was the biggest event that ever hit Riley, Virginia. It was the talk of the town. People huddled outside the church where the ceremony took place to catch a glimpse not only of Quinton, but his superstar teammates who had come to town for the ceremony.

Angela arrived at the church in time to witness the arrival of Taylor Brown in a sleek, white limo with tinted glass. The caramel beauty was dressed in a designer baby blue-colored dress. Her honey blonde hair fell forward in her face, adding to her sensual quality.

Quinton appeared at the door of the church and greeted the woman with a smile and a brief kiss. Then they disappeared inside the building, holding hands as eager fans called out to her.

"Mom, did you see Quinton? He's the man," gushed Tyson with adolescent admiration. "I hope I get a chance to take a picture with Taylor. Quinton promised he would arrange it."

"I'm sure he won't have a problem getting her to do that favor," Angela told her son, hating the jealously she knew she had no right feeling.

As she and Tyson approached the church, she thought of the way Quinton had beamed at the celebrity. Then she thought of how he had dared to ask her out, so that he could get to know her. What in the world would he need with her when he obviously had Taylor sewn up? Maybe he thought that Angela would be more than willing to have a side thing going while Taylor was off touring the country.

Entering the church, Angela and Tyson ran into a harried Quinton. There was no sign of Taylor anywhere. Angela assumed he had tucked the celebrity away until the service to protect her from the scrutiny of her fans.

Quinton beamed at the mother and son. He extended a hand to Tyson. "My man, look at you. A suit and a tie makes you older," he said, taking him by the shoulders and twirling him around in jest to check him out. "I'm going to have to remind all the single women here that you're only thirteen."

Quinton gave a hearty laugh. Then he swung his attention to Angela. The look in his eyes softened at how great she looked in the flattering, wine-colored suit. He stole a quick glance at her high heeled pumps and admired her shapely legs. He studied her face, noting her tasteful makeup. Her sophisticated appearance was appropriate for the day, but he decided that he preferred the Angela who made casual clothes stylish with her voluptuous figure and that touch of class she had acquired in the last few years.

Angela caught him giving her an admiring look and it lifted her spirits. She smiled at him.

"You look great, Quinton. That tux does a lot for you. But I can see the joy you feel for your father in your eyes. That happiness enhances your elegant suit," she said, making an attempt to be cordial.

Grinning, Quinton touched Angela's face. "Thanks for the compliment. It means a lot coming from you."

As a shiver of delight traveled down her spine from his simple touch, Angela tried not to show how she was affected. She grabbed her son by the arm. "We'd better go in and find a seat."

Just as Angela turned to go into the sanctuary, Quinton snagged her by the wrist. "I hope you both plan on attending the reception at the Marriott. Please come," he implored.

Hearing Quinton, Tyson gave his mother a pleading look. "Mom, we've got to go. Uncle Que is going to introduce me to his old teammates. And to Taylor Brown."

Angela smiled wryly. "I completely forgot about all

the celebrities who have come. And I can't let you pass up the opportunity of meeting Miss Taylor Brown," she told her son while looking at Quinton. "We'll be there. My help can take care of the store for one day, I suppose. I hope."

Quinton's mouth relaxed into a smile. "Great. I'm looking forward to dancing with you. So I hope those fancy shoes are comfortable."

Angela laughed softly. "We'll see you later. Shouldn't you be with your father about now?" she asked, fanning him away in a playful manner.

"You're right. I gave him some time alone. He's a bit jittery about his big day," Quinton said. "I better find him now. I'm going to have to show him the ring again to assure him I haven't lost it." He laughed and hurried off down a hallway.

The wedding ceremony between Calvin Gibbs and Beatrice Nixon was beautiful. The sight of the stunning middle-aged couple who even a blind man could tell were in love touched Angela. She thought of how fortunate the two were to have each other. Knowing how Calvin Gibbs had been alone for so long and had raised his children, Angela was glad that he now had someone to enjoy his life with. The couple filled her with hope. Just maybe one day after her son had grown up and moved on, she might find someone to share her golden years.

Once the service was over, she and Tyson hung

around for a while to watch the couple take photographs with family and friends. More people hung around the sanctuary to watch Quinton and his celebrity friends and of course Taylor Brown. Taylor had sung a beautiful standard love ballad as though she were a songbird. At the end of her song, she had blown a kiss to the wedded couple and to Quinton as well. His eyes twinkled with emotion from the beauty that Taylor's voice and her song had bought to the services.

Angela was glad that she had come to the wedding. She loved watching the Gibbs family. Calvin, Jessica, and Quinton were a close knit family. Seeing Quinton and his sister laughing and talking with the newlywed couple, Angela felt a lump of emotion. Despite the fact that Quinton's mother had deserted the family years before, they had managed to stay together, loving each other without being bitter. Calvin Gibbs had done a good job of rearing two children by himself, Angela mused. She hoped that she would be as successful with Tyson. She pulled her son to her and kissed him on the forehead.

Tyson, who was trying to act grown up, was embarrassed and declared. "Mom, not here." He squirmed away from her, but gave her a smile.

"Come on, they're leaving for the reception. We'd better leave too to get there before them," Angela urged her son who appeared to be distracted. Following the direction of her son's interest, she saw Quinton and Taylor standing together and holding hands. She felt a twinge of jealously.

Quinton glanced toward Tyson and Angela and beckoned them over.

Tyson grabbed his mother's hand. "Come on, Mom. I can't go over there by myself."

Though Angela was reluctant and shy about meeting the celebrity, she followed her son over to where Quinton and Taylor were.

Quinton pulled Tyson in front of him and placed his hands on his shoulders. "Taylor, this young man is Tyson Etheridge. He is a big fan of yours. And this is his mother, Angela Etheridge. Her late husband and I were like brothers," he informed the delicate, petite woman.

Taylor smiled at Tyson and took his hand. "It's nice to meet you, Tyson. I always love meeting my fans."

Tyson stared silently at Taylor as though seeing a vision. He wore a silly expression.

Angela was amused by her otherwise talkative son's reaction. She extended her hand to the young woman who had mesmerized her son with her presence. "I enjoyed your song during the ceremony. It was beautiful. Perfect." Angela admired the young woman's flawless complexion and the lovely sheen of her hair.

Taylor accepted her hand. "Thank you. I had to do my best. Quinton is special in my life. I know how much his family means to him and I wanted to do something that would linger in their minds and hearts." She slid her arm around Quinton's waist and smiled up at him with her eyes twinkling.

Angela caught the look and could see that the couple had been more than just friends to each other. As she observed Taylor's admiration, she noticed that Quinton appeared to be uncomfortable with the young woman's display in front of them.

"We'd better go. They're leaving for the reception," he said, stepping away from Taylor. "Taylor has to leave," he informed Angela and Tyson. "She has to make a flight. She has an MTV taping to prepare for."

Taylor ran her hands through her lustrous hair, looking as though she wanted to be alone with Quinton.

Tyson's eyes widened and he yanked the sleeve of Quinton's jacket.

Quinton leaned down to Tyson. "What's up, buddy?"

Tyson whispered into his ear while his mother and Taylor watched.

Quinton grinned and looked at Taylor. "Would you be so kind as to take a picture with my buddy?"

Taylor took Tyson's hand. "I'd love to. Where is that photographer? Let's go outside where the others are and I'm sure he'll be more than happy to snap us. Excuse us." She led a proud Tyson away from Quinton and Angela.

Quinton chuckled. "Looks as though your son has fallen in love. Look at him strut."

Shaking her head, Angela said, "Not only does she have you, but now she's won my son over too." Angela immediately regretted what she had said. She hadn't

131

wanted to appear as though she cared whether or not Quinton was romantically involved with her.

Quinton ran his finger around the collar of his shirt and didn't respond to her comment. "We'd better get outside. I want to see my dad and my new mom take pictures in front of the church before they leave." He placed his hand on the small of Angela's back to lead her outside.

Stepping fast to keep up with Quinton's strides, she was mindful of his touch that had gone from her back to her hand. He held it tightly. She hung on to his hand and savored the moments she had been given with him. She knew that once they were outside, he would be surrounded by friends and fans who had come to celebrate with him.

Outside, Quinton left her side to greet and hug friends, family and any other well-wisher who singled him out.

Tyson returned to his mother's side looking dazed and with a smudge of lipstick on his cheek.

Angela shook her head at her son. "I see you got more than your picture taken," she said, squeezing his chin affectionately. She reached for the handkerchief that she insisted he carry inside his jacket pocket and wiped away the lipstick. She handed him the handkerchief and watched him study the lipstick stain that belonged to Taylor before tucking it carefully back in his pocket.

He sighed. "Mom, she is so real. Wait until the guys

see the picture we took. They're going to be so psyched."
His eyes were dreamy.

"They sure will, son," she said, catching a glimpse of
Quinton walking Taylor to her limo. She watched them
smiling at each other. Then she saw Taylor loop her arms
around his neck and place a tender kiss on his lips.
Quinton tenderly touched her face and said something to
her before she vanished inside. Quinton stood watching
it pull away with a look as dazed as her son's had been.

"Mom, come on, we've got to get to the reception.
Mr. Calvin and Miss Beatrice left a long time ago. I don't
want all the food to be gone by the time we get there,"
Tyson said, taking his mother's hand and tugging her
toward the parking lot.

"Tyson, I'm they're not going to run out of food. Stop
rushing me, boy," she urged, feeling a bit irritated,
remembering how Quinton had responded to Taylor as he
saw her off.

Once they were in the car and had pulled out of the
church parking lot, Angela drove past Quinton, who was
strolling toward his jeep with three lanky, well-dressed
men.

Tyson leaned out the window of Angela's car and
waved to Quinton.

"See you at the reception," Quinton called to them as
they passed.

"See you," Tyson said, grinning. He settled back in
his seat. "Mom, all of those guys are NBA players. I

can't believe they've come to Riley. Do you think they'll take pictures with me too?"

"I'm sure Quinton will arrange that for you," she said, keeping her focus on the traffic.

"You can get in on the picture too, Mom. You can put it up in your store and impress your customers. You should have taken a picture with Taylor. She is really cool, Mom." He wore a dreamy look "She's going to send me some autographed souvenirs. She told me she would give them to Quinton for me. I can't wait," he enthused.

Angela smiled at her son. She was bothered by the fact that listening to her son speak of Taylor stirred up feelings of jealously. She had met the young woman and she had seen Quinton with her. Though he had told her he wasn't seriously involved with Taylor, she could see that there was some chemistry between them. And she could tell that Taylor wanted Quinton. He might not have been emotionally involved with her now, but Angela had a feeling that Taylor was the kind of woman who knew how to get what she wanted.

As she and Tyson neared the Marriott Hotel, she looked in her rearview mirror and saw that Quinton and his crew of friends were behind her. Seeing him sitting behind the wheel of his car struck a vibrant chord in her that she didn't want to feel. The more she saw Quinton or was around him, the more she was becoming entranced. He made her feel the way her son felt with his crush for

Taylor Brown. Angela didn't want to experience warm feelings for Quinton. At thirty-two, she didn't have the courage to get involved with a man like Quinton who had all kinds of women at him. She would be asking for trouble. But her heart was restless and she hadn't forgotten how wonderful Quinton had made her feel that night she had surrendered to his charm.

Though Angela had been reluctant to attend the reception, the moment she entered the lavishly decorated room that bustled with people and the sound of a live band that rocked classic R & B from the fifty and sixties, she was glad she had come. She had a chance to see people she hadn't seen in the last couple of years. She was pleased when she finally had an opportunity to speak with Quinton's father and his bride, who insisted she call her Beatrice. Midway through the reception, Quinton's sister Jessica took the time to chat with Angela to make her feel as though she were one of the family. Angela thought Jessica looked radiant in her gold matron-of-honor dress. Though Jessica and Angela had met while Cole was alive, neither of them had taken the time to get to know one another.

Jessica greeted Tyson with a hug. "You look so handsome today, buddy," she told him. Then she said to Angela, "I'm so glad that you and Quinton have settled your differences. You can't imagine what it has meant to him to be able to see Tyson again."

Tyson wiggled out of Jessica's arms. "Jessica, I want

to get something else to eat and I want to be nearby when they cut that big cake."

Laughing softly, Jessica released him. "Go on. Save some for the rest of us,"she called after Tyson as he hustled away. "My goodness I can't get over how he's grown. He's so much like Cole."

Angela sighed. "That he is," she agreed. "He is the spitting image in the looks department." She smiled at Jessica. "It was a beautiful ceremony. Your father has gotten himself a lovely woman as a wife."

"Girl, I'm so happy that he has her. I worried about him so much. Now he has someone to share his life with. Someone who not only has his same interests, but someone who loves him and appreciates what a great man he is. He's been lonely for so long. He always made Quinton and me his priority. Quinton and I are happy for him. It's way past time for him to enjoy his life. Now if only I could find a good woman for my brother."

Angela sipped on her glass of champagne. "Taylor and Quinton are an item, aren't they?" she asked, trying to mask her curiosity.

"Oh please, girl. Taylor is talented and she's beautiful, but she's not what my brother needs," Jessica responded. "Just like any man, he is fascinated by her twenty something beauty and her sensuality, but there's not much to her. I don't think she's the kind of woman he can build a future with."

Angela listened to Jessica and agreed with what she

said though she didn't verbalize it. "They make a nice couple. I saw them together after the wedding and they looked rather cozy."

Jessica leaned close to Angela and gave her a knowing look. "Angela, you've been married. You know that all those two have together is probably hot sex." She chuckled. "But when the passion dies, my brother's interest will fall upon someone else. My celebrity brother has no trouble getting women. If only he could find someone to settle down with." Jessica's attention was diverted by the sight of her daughter who had been the flower girl. She gasped when she noticed that her daughter had spilled punch on the front of her frilly dress. "Look at that," Jessica exclaimed. "We still have more pictures to take. I'd better take her to the restroom to see if I can remove that stain." She jumped to her feet. "We'll talk again soon, I hope. Please don't be a stranger. You're welcome in our home any time."

"Thanks," said Angela. "And the same goes for you. Stop past my store when you're in the neighborhood. Come browse and have a cup of tea with me."

"That's sounds wonderful. Well, I'd better take care of my daughter and make sure that everything else is taken care of. It's just about over." She exhaled as though to relieve herself of her weariness.

Angela sat listening to the music and watching the guests dance the electric slide. She was amused when she saw Tyson on the floor and keeping in step with everyone else. She'd had no idea he knew how to do the dance.

"Now, why are you just sitting here while everyone else is having fun?" Quinton asked, coming near Angela. "Get up out of that chair, lady. Come on and get in on the action." He took her hand in his and led her to the dance floor.

Angela felt self-conscious. She couldn't remember the last time she had danced. And she didn't know if she could do that line dance the way everyone else could. "Quinton, I have two left feet," she said, giving him a helpless look.

"Don't worry. You can't mess this up. Just relax and follow what I do." Quinton placed his hands on her waist and proceeded to dance, encouraging her to follow his moves.

At first, Angela was mechanically imitating his steps. But she soon found herself feeling the rhythm and getting the steps down.

Seeing how the joy of the music lighted her face and caused her to move her hips more sensually filled Quinton with delight. He loved seeing Angela, who had seemed so guarded, so conservative, letting her hair down and having a good time.

They stayed on the floor for a while dancing to the upbeat numbers. Then the band announced that they were playing the newlywed couple's favorite song, a love ballad of everlasting love and devotion, for them to dance to before they made their getaway to begin their honeymoon and life as Mr. and Mrs. Calvin Gibbs.

Everyone cleared the floor to watch Calvin and his bride take the floor and dance to their song.

Quinton took Angela by the hand and led her off the dance floor. They stood on the side, watching the couple. Quinton moved behind Angela and placed his hands on her shoulders.

A cozy warmth consumed her from Quinton's nearness. His hands were warm and she was titillated by the fragrance of his cologne. Suddenly she felt Quinton's arms around her waist. He whispered in her ear, "I'm so glad my old man has found someone special."

The feel of his breath fanning her ear sent a wave of desire through her. She laughed nervously and moved away, then turned to face him. "They are a beautiful couple," she said. She rubbed the back of neck, feeling flushed. "Excuse me," she told him, "I'd better see what my son is up to. I haven't seen him for a while."

Quinton smirked. "Tyson is fine. He met up with a pretty classmate of his. Some young lady named Mia. The last time I saw him in was in the hall, making eyes with her."

This bit of news made Angela curious. "I'd better check on him," she said, anxious to be away from Quinton and the way he could make her feel.

Reaching the hallway, Angela found her son talking to a girl who appeared to be older than he was. She had a fully developed figure and a bosom that was larger than hers, Angela noticed. She walked over to Tyson. "I was wondering where you had gotten," she said. "Are you ready to leave?"

"No, not yet, Mom," Tyson said, blinking the way he did when he was nervous.

The young lady stood smiling politely.

"Hello, I'm Tyson's mother, Mrs. Etheridge. Who are you?" she asked in a friendly tone.

"I'm Mia Davis," the young girl said in a soft tone.

"Nice to meet you," Angela said. "Do you two go to the same middle school?" she asked, admiring Mia's dimples.

"Mia and I are in the same homeroom," Tyson said. He wouldn't look at his mother.

Angela sensed that she was intruding on her son's attempt to be friendly with the girl. She decided to return to the reception. "Don't go far. We'll be leaving soon," she told him. "See you, Mia."

Entering the reception hall, Angela was hit by the band's singer, crooning another romantic oldie ballad. She had heard the particular song often on the oldies station that she had grown found of listening to at night on the "Quiet Storm" radio program. She felt lonely and out of place. Everyone was paired with someone. Her own son had something going on with Mia.   She felt a little older, realizing that her baby was at the age where he found girls attractive.

Quinton strolled up to her and chided, "Angela, we're supposing to be celebrating. Come on. You owe me a dance." He took her by the hand and led her to the dance floor as the male singer crooned a song she knew by name, "Your Precious Love." She loved the classic with its heartrending lyrics. Meeting the kind and caring expression on his handsome face, Angela welcomed the excuse to dance with him. The minute that Quinton swung her into the circle of his arms, her heart began to race. Her concerns over dealing with her adolescent son's crush faded. She looked into Quinton's eyes and was no longer Tyson's mother, just a woman who needed a man like Quinton to lean on, to make her appreciate her femininity and the importance of the sexuality that she had denied herself. Relaxing in his embrace, she felt heat radiating from his strong body. The song lyrics which spoke of being cherished and loved by one man made her forget the boundaries that she wished to keep with Quinton. As Quinton pulled her closer to him and held her hand tighter, Angela rested her face on his chest. She closed her eyes, feeling comforted and invulnerable. Swaying to the tender ballad, Angela felt as though no one existed but herself and Quinton.

Angela regretted the end of the song. Glancing up at Quinton, she noticed a dreamy look that matched the way she felt. Smiling at him, she could barely breathe. When he caressed the side of her face and leaned in to kiss her lips, she didn't resist the gift. She welcomed the affection and the heady sensation. Though the kiss was brief, it had a lingering sensation. She licked her top lip to cool the heating effect it had on her. She smiled as though she were high off a drug.

As they stood in the middle of the dance floor while others danced to a different song, Quinton took her arm and pulled her to him to whisper in her ear. "Give us a chance, Angela. There's no sin in the attraction we have for each other. Let me come to your place after I'm done with this wedding business. We can talk about any concerns or fears you might have."

Angela struggled with her emotions and the yearning in her heart. Then her voice came out in a hushed tone. "Sure...we can talk. Don't come until midnight. Tyson should be asleep by then," she suggested, peering into his warm eyes that contained a sensuous flame. She felt enraptured. "Uh, I wouldn't want Tyson...well, you understand."

A grin overtook his handsome creamy-chocolate face. "Sure, I understand. Midnight will be fine." He squeezed her hand and gave her an adoring look.

The wonderful spell between them was broken when Quinton's sister Jessica dashed up to him. "Quinton, come with me. Dad and Miss Bea are all set to leave for their honeymoon. They want to talk privately with us before they make their getaway," she urged before hurrying away toward someone who called her.

Quinton released Angela's hand. "Tonight," he said

with a look of promise.

She nodded, feeling her heart race from excited anticipation.

He winked at her, turned on his heel and strolled away to find the newlyweds.

Watching his confident stride as he left, she ignored the cynical voice in her head that told her she was treading on dangerous ground. Instead, she went with the glow in her heart that made her want to forget being rational or doing what was proper and fitting. Quinton had made her want to satisfy her craving to be a complete sexual woman. She had denied herself these feelings for so long that now she felt as though she would burst if she didn't release the passion that brewed deep in her soul. The thought of being alone with Quinton sent a hot flash through her. Tyson dashed up to her. "Mom, come on. They're getting ready to leave. I've got bubbles for us," he said, handing his mother one of the tiny bottles of bubble solution he had. She accepted the bottle that all the guests had been given to wish the couple well as they made their getaway and grabbed her son by the hand. "We'd better hurry," she said, giggling with a joy she hadn't felt in a long time. She knew that Quinton would be outside as well and she could get one last glimpse of him before she and Tyson left for home. She was glad that she had agreed to see Quinton later. Though she had no idea what tomorrow would bring, tonight she wouldn't be lonely or alone. She refused to think about Quinton's unclear involvement with Taylor. Tonight there was a promise of bliss. That was all she needed—just for today and tonight.

Chapter 8

Since arriving home from the fabulous event, Angela had spent the time worrying and wondering if she had done the right thing by agreeing to let Quinton visit. Enchanted by the mood of the moment when they danced to the oldies ballad, she had wanted to see him and to be alone. She wasn't ashamed to admit to herself that she was sexually attracted to him. The last few years of her marriage to Cole had been passionless and lonely ones. Cole had married her when she had gotten pregnant. It hadn't been out of love, but obligation. At nineteen that had been enough for her. Naively, she had believed that she could transform his sense of responsibility into love. To everyone who lived in Riley and saw them out as a family they'd had a solid marriage. She had lived a lie in order to hold her home together for her son, who had been important to both of them.

When Quinton arrived promptly at midnight, her doubts and fears were allayed. The moment he strolled into her house, her heart bubbled with joy and every fiber of her being felt alive.

"What a day," he exclaimed, following her into her family room and removing his jacket, tossing it on a nearby chair. "I've never seen my dad happier. That's what it's all about. My sister and I did our best to make everything as perfect as we could for Dad and Miss Beatrice." He dropped down on the leather sofa and studied Angela, who looked appealing dressed in a simple white sweat suit. Her black hair hung straight and fell into her face, giving her a sensual look. She was gorgeous, he thought, trying to maintain his focus.

Even though she sat on the other end of the sofa, she could still smell the distinctive scent of his cologne. His complexion glowed as though he had just freshly showered. "Everything was lovely," Angela agreed, feeling giddy with his presence. "I'll bet you're worn out from all the entertaining and the guests who came to be with you today."

He turned toward her and gave her a dazzling smile. "Far from it. I'm sort of high from all the positive energy of the day. I'm glad that you invited me over. I'd probably spend the night too wired to sleep." He gave her an easy smile.

His smile sent her pulses racing. And she remembered how good she'd felt in his arms, standing close to his well-defined body earlier that day. She had to move away from him. She jumped to her feet. "How about some wine? You can turn the radio off and play some CDs," she suggested, leaving the room to take a break from the aching feelings of desire she had for him.

Before she prepared a tray with the wine and glasses, she leaned against the refrigerator door. She inhaled and exhaled to calm the beating of her heart and the burning desire that consumed her. After she composed herself, she opened the fridge and got the wine, then found some cheese and crackers. Quinton was a family friend, she told herself. Her husband's best buddy. He was her son's mentor. More than enough reasons not to get intimate with him. But then she had looked in his eyes while they danced. Her heart had been ignited and her body had a craving that had left her restless, yearning for passion. Staring into space, she thought of Quinton's ambiguous relationship with Taylor. Another reason not to let things get out of hand. She picked up her tray and wheeled to return to the family room. As she entered the room, Quinton who sat on the floor going through her CD rack, looked at her and flashed a grin that made his eyes appear to sparkle. Angela's mind clouded and she decided to forget all the reasons not to get involved and listened instead to her heart and her body tell all the reasons to be only a woman who wanted to held and adored.

She and Quinton spent the next hour sipping wine,

listening to jazz and talking over certain humorous events of the wedding.

Angela hugged a pillow with her legs folded on the sofa, striking a pose that caused Quinton to give her lingering looks. He reached over and took the pillow from her and took her hand. "Enough about the wedding. Let's talk about us."

Holding on to his hand and eyeing him intensely, Angela was filled with a sense of urgency. "Where do we begin, Quinton? I mean, we have so many things to get past before we can even consider us."

"That's why I'm here. I'm hoping that we can find a starting point that is comfortable for you," he said, squeezing her hand.

Taking a deep breath, Angela said, "I want to clear the issues from the past I have with you. When Cole was alive and our marriage hit rock bottom, I believed you had a big part in driving us apart."

Quinton frowned and released her hand. He sat forward and grew pensive. "Believe me, I never encouraged Cole's whoring around. Sure, I knew of it. But I never arranged any dates for him. He and I had several arguments because I kept trying to get him to see he had everything he needed at home."

"But Quinton, I caught him with that woman in your house in your bed. I got a phone call late at night from some woman, telling me I could find my husband in your house." Angela spoke in a quiet, angry tone.

"Think back, Angela. Remember that was during basketball season. That night that you showed up at my place ready to throw a fit, I had just returned home for a few days. I had only been home a few minutes when I found that Cole had been...uh, entertaining. I was as pissed as you. Then you showed up, refusing to listen to reason. You pushed past me and walked in my house to catch Cole in bed with that woman. You accused me of harboring him. You wouldn't listen to reason. You cursed me and told me I wasn't welcome in your home or near Tyson anymore. You punished me for Cole's behavior."

Hearing him relate the incident that had been a determining factor in her marriage, she felt as though an old wound had been reopened. She turned away from him to hide the hurt and humiliation she had experienced from that time. Finally she spoke. "Cole idolized you. The more successful you became in the NBA, the more dissatisfied he became with himself. Cole started drinking more than he should. And when he did, he reminded me of how I had snuffed all of his dreams by getting pregnant and causing him to drop out of college to marry me and to take care of me and Tyson."

Quinton gave her a sympathetic look . "Cole had no right to blame you for what he never achieved. He needed to take responsibility for the way his life turned out. Cole was my friend, but he was spoiled. His mother and aunt raised him to believe that he was perfect. He had done well in high school, but when we went away to college, the only things that Cole wanted to do were party and to nail every girl whom he could charm."

Angela got a distant look as though she was conjuring up memories of the past. "I remember arriving on campus as a naive freshman and seeing Cole. I had never met a guy who was as fine and as smooth as he. And when he approached me and asked to see me, I felt as though I had won a million dollar lottery. I was an ordinary girl who didn't have much dating experience. The only times I had socialized with guys were at church functions. I didn't have my first real date up until I attended the prom with a safe, nice guy my parents had chosen for me." A look of amusement came into Angela's eyes. "Guys were leery of dating a preacher's daughter. My father was the pastor of one of the largest African-American churches in West Virginia. My parents had been strict with me. They set an example for the other parents in the church by the way they raised my older sister Karen and me. My sister made them proud. She graduated from college in English and got a master's and then a doctorate. She taught at Howard University until she married. I, on the other hand, disgraced my family and ruined my father's credibility as a preacher by getting pregnant my first semester in college before my nineteenth birthday."

"But you did get married," Quinton said.

She sighed and nodded. "I adored him and loved

him. He was my first love. I believed that despite the way
our marriage began that we were going to have a happy
life. However, after Tyson came, he became his priority.
Tyson was his blood. Whenever he held him or was near
him, the affection for his son was evident. But our marriage never really blossomed and grew the way a marriage should. Though I wanted more children, he made
sure that we had no more. I used to blame myself for our
marriage not working. I wanted us to be happy, but I
couldn't do it all on my own. Right before his death, I
was drained emotionally and wanted to be away from
him. I just couldn't take living without love or respect.
After I learned the way he was dating behind my back as
though our marriage or I meant nothing to him, I knew it
had to be me." She looked embarrassed that she had
been such a failure in her marriage.

Quinton scooted closer to her and placed his arm
around her shoulder. "As much as I loved Cole, I have to
admit that he treated you terribly. He couldn't have had
a better woman than you for his wife and a mother to his
child. It was his misfortune that he couldn't appreciate
you." Tenderness glimmered in his eyes.

She welcomed that expression and was warmed by
it. She placed her hand on his and smiled weakly, feeling
her heart drumming from his sincerity, his empathy.

As they sat staring at each other, she was fascinated
by his sexual magnetism. She lowered her eyes from his
to quell the feelings.

Quinton ran his finger slowly along the side of her face and encouraged her to look at him. "You are special, Angela. Don't ever let anyone ever make you feel any less than that," he said in a tone full of awe and respect.

His sincerity bought tears to her eyes; her heart quivered; she became mesmerized, transported to a zone where no one mattered but him and her.

His hand rested on the back of her neck and he pulled her toward him to give her a slow, thoughtful kiss. Angela relished the feel of his warm and moist kiss. She was so excited by the kiss that she grew slightly breathless. Then he enfolded her in his arms and settled back on the sofa. His kisses grew more urgent, more heated. The firmness of his lips and the lock of his embrace melted the small bit of restraint she had been trying to hold on to. She wound her arms around his back and surrendered passionately to his kiss. Their lips meshed together, sending her temperature soaring. His tongue traced her full sensual lips and then parted them, probing the recesses of her mouth. His forceful tongue caressed hers, setting her core aflame with desire. His hand was beneath her sweatshirt and fondling one of her breasts. She caught her breath, grabbed his hand and sat up. She breathed deeply, licked her lips that had been singed by his kiss. Was she really ready to go to the next level with him? She wanted him, but she wondered if she was strong enough to give herself physically without entangling her emotions. She knew women who could do just that. But she had had only one lover in her entire life. And that man, her husband, had made her feel that she hadn't been enough woman for him. Now she had this fine, sexy man who treated her as though she was the most enticing creature he had ever been with. She more than liked the way he made her feel. But could one adventurous interlude end up complicating her life? Quinton sat up beside her, draped his arm around her shoulder and pressed his forehead to hers. "It's okay. Give in to the feelings, Angela," he implored. He kissed the side of her face; he buried his face in her neck and breathed a kiss there.

She felt the heady sensation of his lips against her neck. She wanted him badly. With a trembling hand, she touched his face and kissed him with a hunger that belied her fears and doubts. Ending the kiss, she embraced him and whispered in his ear, "We'll be more comfortable in my bedroom."

Giving her a smoldering look, Quinton jumped to his feet and pulled her off the sofa. "Lead the way," he said in a velvety tone, intertwining his fingers with hers.

She led the way to her bedroom that she had shared with no other man than her husband. Her heart swelled with emotions she had thought never to know again.

Once they were inside her bedroom, Angela locked the door. She didn't want to risk Tyson wandering in and finding her with Quinton. As she whirled around, Quinton was on her. He pinned her to the closed door with his body, giving her deep, passionate kisses. As he kissed her, his hands went beneath her sweatshirt and sought the hook in the back of her bra and unfastened it. Quick as a flash, his hand cupped her full breasts and thumbed the nipples while he kissed her behind her ear. Angela squirmed from his delightful touches. Knowing how much he wanted her made her feel even more sexy and bold. She wanted to make this night one that would last in her mind and her heart. She had no idea when she would have the courage to venture into such a sexual escapade again. For all she knew, this would be a one night stand. Though Quinton seemed sincere, he could only be taking advantage of vulnerability that she knew she reeked of whenever he was near. But for tonight that was okay. She wanted him to use her and she certainly hoped to use him in order to feel alive, to feel like a desirable woman from head to toe.

She interrupted his ardent affection and pushed him toward the queen-sized bed that she had slept in alone for so long. Holding the glowing look in his extraordinary eyes, she gave him a teasing smile. Pushing him down on the foot of the bed, she stepped away from him and proceeded to remove her clothes under his intense scrutiny. She tugged her sweatshirt over her head and tossed it aside, then snatched away her loosened bra and added it to the heap of her garments. To tease him further, she turned her back to him and eased her sweat pants slowly down over her curvaceous bottom, her luscious thighs and shapely legs, kicking them aside. By the time she turned to face a silent, captivated Quinton, she found him hustling out of his clothes. He had removed his shirt and had begun to unbuckle his belt. She sauntered up to him and smacked his hands away so that she could do the chore for him.

Giving him a blazing look, she undid the belt, unfastened his slacks and eased down the zipper of his fly, letting the pants fall to the floor. She stepped closer to him and wrapped her arms around his waist and pressed her face against his chest. He ran his fingers through her hair and onto the warm flesh of her shoulders and down her back, to her behind. While one hand rested on her bottom, he gripped the back of her neck and tilted her head to claim her lips with a crushing kiss. Her hands slid inside the back of his boxers. She placed her hands on his firm buttocks and caressed him. His impressive manhood rose and peeked out of the slit in front of his underwear, brushing against her body. She liked the feel of his arousal upon her flesh; she snatched down his boxers to free him even more.

Quinton's eyes glimmered with approval. He chuckled softly and pulled her against his nudity, holding her and caressing her shapely body as though enchanted by her. He licked her lips, her eyelids and the tip of her nose. Then he swept her into his arms and carried her to the bed and placed her there. She pulled back the covers, climbed beneath them and made room for him.

Without any hesitation, he met her there. Beneath the covers, they came together in a tangle of arms and legs. As they engaged in a hot tongue kiss, Quinton moaned with pleasure, cradling her exquisite form to him. Angela shivered. She had forgotten the thrills of intimacy. She had forgotten what it was like to feel so many sensations at one time. Quinton moved on top of her. At once, he rewarded her with lingering caresses and tender kisses all over her body. She arched her body upward toward him as he sought her breasts, fondling them and thumbing her nipples until they were hard. He amazed her by the way he tasted her nipples as though they were gourmet chocolate morsels. The feel of his lips and his tongue there sent jolts of pleasure to her center, causing her to throb and grow moister still. She breathed deeply to cool her fevered body and slow her trembling heart. However, she grew warmer still when she felt his hand between her thighs, on her mound, and then his long, skillful fingers probing her in a manner that made her hum softly from the gratification he inspired. Filled with anxious anticipation and aching to be filled with his passion rod that had pressed against her flesh and titillated her all the while he lavished her with his sweet intimate consideration, she parted her legs.

He knelt between her legs and hovered over her, licking first one breast then another. Then his wonderful mouth seared a slow path downward to her navel. She squirmed beneath him and gripped his shoulders and let out a cry of delight.

Quinton caressed her dewy center before burying his fully erect and condom-covered arousal deep inside her.

The moment that they were joined together, tears leapt into Angela's eyes. He made her feel alive and like a complete woman. As his hard body massaged her with a slow, entrancing rhythm, she wrapped her legs around his hips and relished his steady thrusting. She matched his moves by swaying her hips in tandem to his. Taken to paradise, she closed her eyes and relished the moment. She caressed the tendons in the back of his neck and lowered her hands to the muscular rippling on his back.

Moaning in excitement, he and she became erotic athletes. She responded with a rhythm and ferocity that matched his all-consuming eagerness. She grew wild beneath him, unleashing all the pent-up desire she had been harboring. Soon there was a dizzying uprush of emotion that she couldn't restrain. She dug her nails into his shoulders and surrendered to the swirl of sensations that seized her center and spread to her heart. Quinton picked up the tempo to a savage fierceness that carried him, then her, to a full, joyous climax. The last delicious, shuddering moments came on them simultaneously. Exchanging tender glances at that ultimate moment only intensified the pleasure, making them feel as though they were drowning from the rapture they shared. Unleashing joyful cries, Angela clung to him, feeling peace and a satisfaction that was indescribable. Exhausted, Quinton rested on her breasts before seeking her lips to share sweet kisses that made her shiver even more. Weary from their satisfying lovemaking, they fell into a lover's nap.

Angela awoke locked in Quinton's arms. At first, she thought she had dreamed the wondrous lovemaking with Quinton, her late husband's friend, her son's mentor. As her mind cleared from her drowsiness, she knew that it had all been real. She wiggled cozily in his arms and glared at the clock on her nightstand and saw that it was six a.m. in the morning. Then reality hit her. She thought of her son and bolted upright in bed and turned to shake Quinton awake.

Quinton stirred and blinked at Angela, easing his mouth into a slow smile. He took hold of her arm, yanked her down on him and started kissing her. "Some night, huh?" His hands caressed the curve of her waist, her hips. Then he rolled on top of her, layering her neck with kisses.

Angela delighted in his affection. He stoked a gently growing fire that she found delightful. She looped her arms around his neck and looked into in his eyes, trying to ignore the feel of his arousal pressing against her mound. "It was sweet," she admitted in a soft tone.

Quinton rested his forehead against hers and pressed his chest to her breasts and shifted his shoulders, brushing her nipples gently, attempting to seduce her. "To say it was sweet hurts my ego. I'd like to think of it as hot, mind blowing or better yet, that I rocked your world, lady." He traced her sensuous lips with the tip of his tongue before kissing and nibbling at them.

It took everything in her to halt his amorous affection. She pushed at him. "Quinton, you've got to go. I can't risk Tyson waking up and finding us like this." She rolled from beneath him and scooted out of bed.

Quinton sat up and tossed back the covers, bringing a knee up, and stared at Angela. "I suppose you're right."

Angela whirled and faced him. The sight of him looking handsome and sexy made her heart spin with the kind of affection she was scared to claim. Noticing how his glance lingered on her body, she suddenly became self-conscious about her nudity. She turned to her closet where she kept her bathrobe, snatched it off the rack, slipped it on and wrapped it around her.

Amused, Quinton climbed off the bed and stood stretching as if to show off his marvelous body. "Too late for modesty, isn't it?" His eyes twinkled with mischief.

She beamed at him and her mood was buoyed by his reluctance to leave. She bent and reached for his clothes that lay in a heap by the side of her bed. When she did, Quinton eased up behind her and fitted his hands around her waist and turned her to face him.

"When can we get together again?" he asked, locking his hands at the base of her back and pulling her against his nudity.

159

Angela couldn't hold his gaze. "I don't know. There are so many things to consider," she said thoughtfully.

Quinton's pleasant expression turned pensive. "What's there to consider? You and I have something going on that's..."

Angela refused to allow herself to get entangled in a commitment. She shook her head. "You and I had sex. That's all," she said, as though she were trying to convince her heart and her mind. She shoved the clothes she had gathered at him and moved away.

"Come on, Angela. It was more than that. You know it," he said, staring at her.

"I can't buy that. I can't afford to. You have something with Taylor Brown. She's a celebrity with a busy schedule. She doesn't have time to play with you and so, you probably feel as though I can help fill up that time when she's away," she said. "Last night was fine. But, I know that you and I don't stand a chance."

"The only reason why we wouldn't be able to make it is because you don't want to. I have told you that Taylor and I aren't that close." Scowling, he grabbed his shorts and slacks from the tangle of clothes and dropped his other things on the end of the bed. He stepped into his shorts and then his slacks, eyeing Angela, who leaned against her dresser with her arms folded. Her remarks cut him, made him feel as though he had been used as some kind of mindless stud.

Angela had enjoyed every minute of their lovemaking. Yet her wonderful feelings of shared pleasure were smothered with guilt. Heaven forbid that her son should suspect this intimate friendship, she mused with anxiety. How would she explain to Tyson who thought the world of his father that she was interested in the man who was his father's best friend, the man he thought of as an uncle. It was too much for her already confused and troubled son to deal with. As far as Tyson was concerned, he was the only man she needed to protect her. Hadn't he always promised his father that he would look after her? She dared to think what learning that his mother had sexual needs like any other woman would do to him.

"Quinton, it was nice. But it mustn't happen again. You have a life and I'm a mother. My son is my priority. And I have my bookstore to keep me busy. That's more than enough for me."

Quinton was fully dressed. He shook his head. "That's not the kind of life a healthy young woman should live. You have to talk to Tyson about life and make him understand that you need more. You can't let him grow up with you pretending to be someone that you aren't. He'll understand women better if he knows the kind of needs his mother has. It won't make him respect you any less if you talk to him in a straightforward manner."

Angela considered Quinton's words. Could he be right? she wondered, considering the astounding sexual

satisfaction she'd shared. It would be great to have someone such as Quinton with such prowess in her life. She
dismissed the thought quickly. She wasn't ready to take
that kind of risk with her son. Maybe when the boy was
older. Right now, she was just pulling him out of a rebellious stage. She didn't want to go back to that because of
a man. Integrating any man, especially Quinton, into her
life would create far too many complications.

"Too much of a risk. If you were a parent, you'd
understand," she said finally. She walked to the door to
escort Quinton out of her bedroom, her home, and her
life.

Quinton halted her by snagging her by the wrist and
staring into her eyes. "Think about this. Say you'll do
this. We could have something if you'd just give it a
chance. We could work with Tyson and..."

Looking into Quinton's heavenly eyes, she was
affected. Was he really worth all the trouble he would
bring into her simple and ordinary life? she wondered.
"I'll think about it, but I can't make any promises," she
said, moving away from him. She knew she would never
forget the night of passion they'd shared and she knew
that now she would be lonelier than before because she
had known what it felt like to lie beneath him and to feel
his comforting warmth, his body close to hers. She threw
open her bedroom door for Quinton.

Before exiting, Quinton placed a hand on the side of
her face and gave her a lingering kiss on her lips.

She closed her eyes and gave in to the tantalizing sensation.

"Mom! Uncle Que!" exclaimed a drowsy and confused-looking Tyson who stood in the hallway.

Angela was mortified by her son's sudden appearance. She stepped away from Quinton and toward Tyson. But before she could say anything or even reach for him, he fled to his room and slammed his door. Her shoulders slumped and her face burned with shame.

Quinton leaned in her bedroom doorway, looking as defeated as Angela did. "We should talk to him," he said in a thoughtful tone.

"And tell him what? That you and I spent the night together, rolling in the bed that I shared with his father?" she snapped.

"We're adults. He's not a child. He's old enough to understand..."

"I'm his mother. How can I maintain his respect now that he knows I've had a sleepover with you?" she said in an accusatory tone. She leaned against the wall, biting her lip as tears spilled from her eyes.

Quinton sauntered over to her. "It's going to be all right. You're making too much out of this. I think this is a perfect time for us to let him know how we really feel about each other." He reached for her to comfort her in his arms.

Angela recoiled from his touch. "There's nothing between us," she growled. "Just leave, Quinton. I'll get through this just the way I've had to get through everything before I let you into our lives."

Quinton's looked dismayed, hurt. "Angela, there's no need to act this way. There's nothing to be ashamed of."

"Easy for you to say. You don't have any children. You only have to think of yourself and your needs," she said. She wiped away her tears with the side of her hand. "You'd better leave. I need to be alone. I have to find a way to talk to my son and explain things in a way that he can still respect me."

"Angela, let me help..."

"No! The only way you can help is by leaving and not coming back any more. I think you and I have done a good job of losing the trust that Tyson had in both of us." She gave him a cold stare that showed she couldn't be persuaded by anything he said or did.

Quinton's brow wrinkled with vexation. "Okay. Fine. If that's the way you feel, so be it. I won't bother you any more." He took off down the hall to the front door and exited in a fury.

Angela stood watching him and feeling lonelier than she ever had. The one night of pleasure she had stolen had turned her world upside down. She had to figure out a way to make it all right and ordinary again. But now that she had lain with Quinton and felt the power of his affection, his loving, she knew that she would never again be content with her old life.

Chapter 9

The moment that Quinton left Angela hustled off to the shower. She felt the need to rinse away any evidence of her shame for her wanton night of pleasure. She wanted her son to understand that she hadn't changed. That she was still his devoted mother, the woman who loved him, that his well-being was foremost in her mind.

Once she had showered and dressed, she felt ready to confront her son. While she dressed, she had heard television in the family room blasting the cartoon network. Knowing that Tyson was up early and watching cartoons was a sign that he was troubled. Usually her son slept late on the weekends. But he had broken his routine this particular morning. He had been up in time to catch her making out with Quinton. Obviously, he had seen

Quinton's car parked in the driveway and was curious as to why he was at their house so early, Angela reasoned. She imagined the confusion and the betrayal her son had felt when he had seen them together.

Entering the room where Tyson lay stretched out on the sofa with his hands behind his head, watching television, Angela was taken aback. Tyson wore one his father's favorite sweatshirts. She had given Tyson some of his father's t-shirts and sweatshirts as keepsakes. She knew that while at the time they were too large for the small boy, it would only be a matter of time before he would grow to fit them. She had hoped that wearing them would give him comfort and keep his father's memory close to his heart. On this morning he wore the navy blue sweatshirt that was still too large for him. Wearing her husband's shirt on this particular morning was probably his way of reminding her that no man should be allowed to take his father's place.

Angela went to the television that was too loud and turned the volume down. "Tyson, you and I need to talk," She went to the sofa where he lay with a blank expression and took hold of his feet to shift them to the floor to make room for her to sit.

Tyson made no response nor did he look in his mother's direction.

Aggravated by his aloofness, Angela grabbed the remote control that rested on his chest and flipped off the television. "Sit up," she ordered. "You and I have to talk."

Tyson sat up slowly. But he wouldn't look at her.

With mixed emotions, she began. "I'm embarrassed that you saw...found Quinton with me. He and uh...we did something that we both regret and..."

Tyson turned toward his mother with contempt in his eyes. "So what if Uncle Quinton is doing you," he said. "I don't care." He reached for the remote control.

Angela seized it. "Wait a minute. It's not like that at all. Quinton and I won't be seeing each other again."

"Good," he snapped. "I'm glad. I thought he cared about me. I was glad that he was around for us." He pouted, "But, we don't need him. You can't let him use you, Mom. I don't care who he is or what he was to Dad." Angry tears gleamed in his eyes. Then he bolted off the sofa and marched off to his room.

Alone, Angela felt a sinking feeling of despair. Her selfish desire for Quinton had hurt her son terribly. She had no idea how she was going to set things right with him. She worried what Tyson might do to act out the repulsion he felt about his mother having feelings like any other woman. She couldn't turn to Quinton for help. Doing so would only make the situation worse than what it was, she believed.

Unfortunately, in the following days Tyson's behav-

167

ior reverted to what it had been before Quinton had stepped in and gotten him back on the right track. Much to Angela's dismay, Tyson had started to hang around the boys who had gotten him in trouble at the mall. In addition, she had gotten a call from two of his teachers who reported her son's bad attitude and the lack of interest in his studies. Both teachers said that Tyson had become indifferent to anything anyone tried to say to help him.

Angela believed that Tyson's behavior was his way of punishing her for betraying him. She had ruined the friendship, the camaraderie he had enjoyed with Quinton. She knew he was confused by what he knew about her and Quinton. Tyson knew that Quinton had been romantically linked with Taylor Brown, so, this made Quinton look like a player who was obviously using his mother for one thing only. And his mother was letting Quinton do this, he must think. Any way the poor child looked at the situation placed her in a bad light.

It was with this tension between herself and Tyson that she had to face Thanksgiving.

She had invited Miss Viveca, Cole's mother, and his Aunt Nadine to her house. She had extended the invitation to them, knowing that she wouldn't be able to share it with her own family who were far away in Germany. She had been looking forward to entertaining the two ladies. She wanted to show them that she was doing well and that she had indeed been capable of being a working mother, keeping a clean home and raising a son who was well-mannered and doing great in school. And all of this would have been true if only she hadn't been charmed by Quinton and let him into her bed. Though she thought of Quinton often, she hadn't had any contact with him since that night a few days ago. She believed it was best to cut off all ties with him. She had to regain her son's respect and show him that she could be the saintly mother he wanted her to be, the one who found satisfaction in taking care of him, running the house and operating her bookstore.

Thanksgiving Eve, Angela closed All of Our Best early. She had her dinner to think of and she hadn't even taken time to complete the grocery shopping she needed for her meal. Stopping in the crowded supermarket on her way home, she maneuvered her way through the busy market with her cart, seeking to find a can of cranberry sauce and the ingredients to make her son's favorite dessert, sweet potato pie.

As she went down the aisle that she had been directed to, searching for the cranberry sauce, she heard her name being called by the one voice she wasn't ready to hear. She glanced over her shoulder and there was Quinton. She felt her face glow at the sight of him, looking as handsome as ever. Her heart raced and she realized how much she had missed his presence, his smile.

Quinton stood with his hands jammed into his bright, casual designer jacket. "I've been stalking you," he said in a playful tone. "I was at the stoplight when I spotted your car turning toward the store. I wanted to see you. I know I'm the last person you want to see, but I couldn't resist coming in to see you. I've been thinking of Tyson and of course, you, wondering how everything has been." He gave her a look full of longing.

Angela unzipped her coat. She no longer felt the chill from the grim, cold day. She gave him a tremulous smile. "I wish I could say that everything is great. But I can't. Tyson has managed to get in trouble at school with only a few days before it is to let out. I can't get him to talk. He has shut me out. When I'm home, he stays closed up in his room. And unfortunately, he's hanging out with that bunch who got him into all that trouble before. I'm worrying myself to death. Other than that, my life is fine and dandy," she said. Her voice cracked, giving away the stress she was under with her son.

Quinton placed a hand on her shoulder. "Angela, why are you letting him treat you this way? You don't have to take his bad behavior."

Angela flashed him an annoyed look. "What am I supposed to do with him? Take a strap to him? Or should I turn him over to the juvenile court to handle and admit that I'm a poor excuse of a mother?" She exhaled and glanced away from him.

Then she stepped away from his touch. Quinton's eyes dimmed from her rebuttal. "Counseling. Have you considered family counseling? You've done what you can with him. But it's obvious that you haven't been able to reach the source of his problems. Maybe you both need professional help," he said in a kind voice.

She sighed with resignation, then grew pensive. She gave him a look that suggested that he might have touched on something she hadn't dared to consider.

"There's no shame in seeing a therapist," he said in an encouraging tone. "No one will have to know. It can be on a completely confidential basis." He stared at her with concern. "You and Tyson have been through quite a bit in the last few years. Both of you are wounded."

Angela looked defeated. "Tyson isn't going to take to this suggestion too well. The last thing he needs to hear from me is that I think he needs a shrink."

Quinton moved closer to her to talk confidently. "This isn't the place to talk like this. But you won't let me come to your house and you refuse to answer your phone. I'm only trying to help you to set things right. I know what you're going through. I've been there. My whole family went through the same thing you and Tyson are going through when my mother walked away from us. All of us were bitter and ashamed of what happened. My dad tried to fix it, so to speak. But it got to be too much for him. He sought help when he got to drinking more than he should to drown his pain and anger. He got help because he wanted to be of sound body and mind for Jessica and me. We got help as a family and it worked wonders."

She listened intently to his revelation. "But Cole

didn't walk out on Tyson. He died," she said, dreading the thought of convincing her son to go to a therapist.

"True, but the boy has grief. I know. It's buried inside of him. There are certain things he won't discuss about Cole. He shuts down and changes the subject. He misses him. He won't admit this to you, because he feels as though he has to be strong. I think that's why he acts out at school and hangs with those thugs. He doesn't want people to think he's a mama's boy because he doesn't have his old man around for him."

"And I added to his problems by allowing you to spend the night with me. No telling how much harm that has done to him," she added. Her complexion grew flushed from her frustration. She groaned as though in pain. "I suppose I will have to get some kind of counseling for the two of us."

He stared at her full of concern. "Angela, let me come home with you. Let me talk to him and explain about us and..."

Angela leaned away from him. Her face clouded with uneasiness. A confrontation with Quinton and Tyson was just too much for her to deal with now. "That's out of the question now. Let's just leave things the way they are. There is no *we*. There can never be a *we*. Don't you understand? The boy remembers you as his father's best friend. He can't fathom the idea of his father's best buddy and his mother in a relationship. He's too immature to deal with that. He prefers to believe that I'm living with all these grand memories of a fantastic marriage that Cole and I never had. Cole and I lived a lie for that boy because we loved him. And now I must deal with the consequences of that. I certainly will not tell him that his father fell out of love me and that he and I had plans to divorce." Her eyes flashed with her frustration and her confusion.

"You can't handle him on your own. Consider professional help," Quinton warned. "If you love that boy as much as I know you do, you'll get it as soon as possible. Both of you will be stumbling and hurting people unintentionally until you can deal with the issues that you refuse to confront with him."

The harried holiday customers in the store eyed Quinton and Angela with impatience for blocking the aisle and the shelves they needed to get to.

He had given her too much to think about, to deal with. She exhaled loudly and turned away from him. Her anxiety and her humiliation over the lack of control in her life made her feel as though Quinton were patronizing her. "I've got to get my groceries. I have too much to do to stand around, whining and listening to your advice," she said in a firm tone to let him know she had spoken enough on the issue.

Catching the look of despair, Quinton said, "I'm only trying to help. That's all," he said, looking helpless at her defensive attitude.

"I don't need your help any more," she said emphat-

Sinclair LeBeau

ically. "You have a glamorous life that you can fall right back in step with. Are you flying out to be with Ms. Taylor Brown? I heard on the radio that she has just moved into a fabulous apartment in New York," she said in a sarcastic tone to change the subject.

"No, I won't be with Taylor for Thanksgiving. My sister Jessica is having Thanksgiving dinner at her house. My father and his bride will be there. Just a simple family gathering," he explained. "I won't see Taylor until the weekend. She has a concert in L. A. and I promised her that I would come," he said in a matter-of-fact tone.

The information pierced her angry heart with jealousy. She masked her feelings with a smirk. "Well, you enjoy your holiday and your weekend. Give your folks my best," she said too cheerily. She gave up trying to look for the cranberry sauce and shoved her cart away from Quinton.

He came after her, calling out her name. But his act only drew attention to himself. Customers in the store recognized "Sweet Que" and surrounded him to shake his hand, to get autographs.

While he was occupied, Angela abandoned her cart and hustled out of the store. She'd go to another store. She didn't want to give Quinton another opportunity to talk to her or to charm her. He didn't have the right to try to run her life simply because she had lain with him intimately. She wasn't going to repeat that mistake again. Let him find happiness with Taylor. She would only be

174

setting herself up for heartache because there was no way in the world she could compete with the glamorous, sophisticated and filthy rich singer, Taylor Brown. But even knowing that, she still felt depressed and remorseful that a relationship between them didn't stand a chance. She thought of his advice concerning Tyson and herself and considered it briefly. But she wasn't ready to deal with the issue just yet. Hopefully, things would get better on their own. She was sure that once her son was assured that there was nothing between her and Quinton that he would straighten out. At least, she prayed he would.

Since Angela had left the store and sought another one in order to avoid Quinton and her feelings, she arrived home feeling edgy and tired. Entering the house through the kitchen, she stared at the mess Tyson had made in the kitchen and grew angry. Obviously he'd had company and fed them. The bread had been left on the counter, along with the deli meat and open condiments. There were potato chip crumbs and empty soda cans scattered about as well. Several candy wrappers had been left here and there. Once she set down her groceries, she stormed through the house and toward Tyson's room where he had been hiding away to avoid her attempts to have a civil conversation with him. When she tried to open his door, it was locked. Angry and at her wit's end with him and his attitude, she pounded on the door as though she wanted to knock it off its hinges.

"Open this door, boy!" she demanded. "Now, Tyson! I've had enough of you and your foolishness." She pounded some more. "Move it, Tyson. Don't make me get a screwdriver and take it off the hinges."

Angela was taken aback when she heard scuffling and hushed conversation behind the door.

Tyson finally opened the door and cracked it. "What's the matter, Mom?" He looked anxious.

Angela glared at her shirtless son who stood at the door as though hiding something, then shoved him out of the way and entered the room to find his classmate, Mia Davis, pulling her sweater over her head. Angela gave her son and the girl a furious look. "Have you lost your minds? You get out of my house," she told Mia who looked as though she wanted to cry.

Mia grabbed her things and fled from the room.

Angela walked over to her son who had dropped on the foot of his bed. "Tyson, I'm ashamed of you. How long has this been going on? I hope that you and that girl haven't...haven't had sex in my house or anywhere else for that matter." The thought of her thirteen-year-old becoming intimate was something that she didn't even want to imagine. But the thought was obviously on his mind. Hadn't she seen the half-dressed girl in his room? Had they completed the act or had he just attempted to see how far the girl would go with him the way his father had done with her when she was an innocent eighteen-year-old?

Beads of perspiration stood out on his face and he wouldn't answer his mother or even look at her.

His silence angered her. She grabbed him by the arm and yanked him to his feet to make him look at her. She glared at her son and gave him an open-handed slap for being insolent. "I won't have you throwing away your life! You've got to stop this and stop it now!" She began to sob. "Why do you keep hurting me? Why?" she exclaimed, throwing up her hands in exasperation.

Tyson held the side of his face and glared at his mother with tears in his eyes.

Angela shoved the boy on the shoulder. "Don't look at me like that. I'm your mother."

Tyson backed away from her; he wrapped his arms around his body as though he had been hit in the stomach. "You don't care about me. All you care about is that damn store of yours and Quinton," he said, sobbing. "Mom, how could you do Dad's friend? You told me Quinton was coming around to help me, not to do you."

Hearing her son, she felt bereft and desolate. Seeing his pain and what he assumed to be her betrayal to his father's memory, she felt misery searing her heart. She stepped toward Tyson and reached out to him. "Oh baby, you must know that you're the most important person in my life. I only want what's best for you, sweetheart.'

Tyson avoided her touch. His face was crumpled with anguish. "When Uncle Que came back, I was glad. I used to love hearing him tell me things about Dad. It kept me from feeling so...so sad. It's was nice to have a guy to hang out with until..."

"I was wrong. But Quinton is a good man. I've been just as lonely as you. I'm only human and...well that thing with him is done. Anyway, he has that singer, Taylor Brown. Can we put this behind us? You've made mistakes and you've seen that I'm not perfect. Tyson, we're all that each other has. We have to stay together and be strong or else or else..." Angela lowered her head and cried, feeling completely devastated by the situation. At a loss for words and weary, she left Tyson's room. Once she had left, Tyson shut his door and she heard him lock it. She fell against it and cried even more.

Chapter 10

"The dinner was wonderful," Miss Viveca, Cole's mother, told Angela. "With everything you have to do now, you still managed by yourself to prepare a home-cooked feast for Thanksgiving.

Miss Viveca had insisted upon helping Angela clean up in the kitchen while Aunt Nadine and Tyson kept each other company, talking and watching television. Unlike other times, Angela welcomed the help of her mother-in-law. The tall woman with the neatly gray hair seemed to be more relaxed and much easier to be around. She hadn't made one disparaging remark the entire time she had been in Angela's home. Usually, Miss Viveca had something negative to say concerning Angela's life or the improper way she believed she was raising her only grandchild.

"I'm glad that you enjoyed it. The day has been really wonderful," Angela said, though she didn't really feel that way in her heart. The moment she rose she found herself wondering what Quinton was doing. She had even been tempted to call him to hear his voice. She had figured she could use the excuse of wishing him a happy Thanksgiving from her and Tyson. But she decided it was best to let things stay as they were. After all, he had someone.

"Nadine and I have been looking forward to being with you and Tyson. Maybe the two of you will come have Christmas dinner with us," she suggested. "The holidays are a time for families and sharing love." Sadness could be seen in her eyes. "You know, I miss Cole so much during the holidays. I never imagined that my child would go before me. "Her voice broke with emotion. "Cole was a comfort to me. When he was with us, I could look into his eyes, his face and see his father, whom I adored. When Cole was killed, a part of me died too. I was so angry, so hurt. I felt as though God had turned his back on me. But He hadn't. He never does. We all have Tyson, who is a part of Cole and such a joy. Despite his teen problems, I truly believe Tyson is going to turn into a fine Etheridge man."

Angela patted Miss Viveca's hand. She wished she could say that she felt the same way, but she couldn't. Sure, she was sad the way that Cole's life had been cut short and sad that Tyson had to lose his loving father at such a young age, but she couldn't lie and tell Cole's mother that she had loved him the way Miss Viveca had obviously loved the husband she lost when Cole was a child. "Tyson misses his dad too. But you know how children don't talk as openly about their pain. I can tell though. I really believe Tyson's misbehavior is a result of the grief and anger he is just beginning to understand and allowing himself to feel."

"One doesn't get through grieving easily," Miss Viveca said. "Though it's been three years since Cole's death, I'm just beginning to feel again. Of course, I'll always miss my son, but I'm not as angry as I was. Like I said, having Tyson is a comfort. I look at him and I see Cole." She smiled with tears pooling in her eyes. She sighed. "Life goes on. Losing loved ones only shows us that we must treasure each day that we are given."

"You are so right," Angela said, giving her a comforting smile.

Miss Viveca stared at Angela as though she was trying to get her thoughts together. Finally she said, "Dear, I have done a lot of soul searching since Cole's death. I...I know that when you two married I wasn't the kindest mother-in-law. You both were so young to have to give up all your dreams to get married and then to have a child. I had problems with Cole when he went away to college. I was constantly trying to make him into the image of his father. My husband was a bright man who was full of ambition and pride. Roger was a wonderful doctor and everyone who knew him loved him and admired him. He was my one and only love. He was so good to me. It's a shame that enough young couples don't experience the kind of love I knew with that man." Her eyes glowed with the real love she had known.

Angela listened quietly, wishing Cole had been as affectionate and devoted as his father had been to his mother.

Miss Viveca studied Angela's expression. "You and Cole had problems in your marriage. Neither one of you was happy. I know, my dear. I knew a lot of things that you didn't think I knew. Cole acted shamefully during your marriage. I tried talking to him, but the more I did the worst he got."

Angela stared at her mother-in-law with a blank expression, amazed by Miss Viveca's confession. She thought of how through the years this woman had treated her as though she were to blame for Cole's irresponsibility, his inability to stay on a job except for the one that he had as a firefighter which gave him a sense of dignity and accomplishment.

"You see, no mother likes to admit that her child had problems. It's like admitting you were a bad mother," she said. She swallowed hard. "I know I never told you this, but you are a good mother and I noticed how hard you tried to be a good wife to Cole. The way he acted hurt me so badly. His father wouldn't have approved at all. I always believed that if he could have grown up witnessing the love and respect between his father and me, he would have had an example of what made a good marriage." She grew silent. "I was young when I lost my husband. Looking back now, I should have married again. I think it means a lot for a boy to have a man around to show him things and talk to him. And I have been lonely. A woman needs companionship, someone to laugh and cry with when times get rough." She stared at Angela. "You are smart and pretty. You loved Cole. You had his son. You adore him and have made sacrifices for him. Tyson is growing up fast. It's time for you to consider yourself, my dear. Don't try to live your life as a lonely and often bitter woman believing that she is to love only one man."

Angela was utterly surprised by her mother-in-law's advice. She was the last person to expect such empathy from.

"Don't look at me as though you think I've lost my mind. I'm only offering you advice to help you and to make up for all those years I avoided getting close to you. I'm growing. I suppose it's never too late to change your ways." She offered Angela a warm smile.

Relenting to Miss Viveca's sincerity, kindness, Angela hugged the woman. Tears filled her eyes, knowing that they could finally set aside their differences for a relationship she could count on.

Miss Viveca broke their embrace. She grabbed a

napkin to wipe her eyes. "Enough of all of this. Nadine and Tyson are waiting for us to join them in the family room and to serve them dessert. Let's finish cleaning up this kitchen. Then I'll percolate some fresh coffee for us."

Angela wiped away her tears of joy and reconciliation with the back of her hand. "I'll load the dishwasher," she said, feeling as though she had one thing for which to be truly thankful on this day. While they set about their kitchen duties, they laughed and talked as though they had always shared an amiable relationship. Once the kitchen was done, they sliced the sweet potato pie that Angela had made and prepared a tray to serve the coffee and dessert in the family room.

As Miss Viveca arranged the places and forks on the tray, she asked Angela, "What's going on with you and Tyson?"

Angela ceased slicing the pie and licked away the smudge of pie filling on her finger. "What makes you think there's something going on?"

Miss Viveca tilted her head and grinned. "I'm a mother who has had a young son. Tyson is so much like his father when he was his age. I noticed how cool and overly polite he's been to you. Whenever my Cole was mad with me or couldn't have his way, he used to give me the same treatment."

Angela twisted her mouth thoughtfully. She didn't know where to begin. She exhaled and said, "He's trying to be a man before he's ready. That's what the problem is. He is driving me to my wit's end."

"Hmm...is that going on already? Well, he is thirteen and I guess the timing is right for him to be testing you. Teens. It's their raging hormones that cause them to think irrationally, to have mood swings and to just fill your life with heartache and disappointments over their actions." She wore a wistful expression on her cinnamon face. "Cole and I had our bad times when he was a teen. But I blamed myself for being too protective. He wanted to get out and get away from under me, but I was so afraid of harm coming to him from hoodlums in the street. Cole was a good-looking boy and he had all the material things I could give him. It created a lot of animosity among his peers other than Quinton. I was caught up in that social circle thing and Quinton's family lived on the other side of town. His father made a living running that little old corner grocery store. But I later learned that they were all good people. Cole looked up to Quinton's father. He loved being with Quinton's family whenever he could. By the way, Tyson told me he has been spending time with Quinton. I think that's kind of Quinton. But I don't expect anything less from someone like him."

"Yeah, Quinton was spending time with him. But he's a busy man who has a life of his own," Angela said quickly.

"Pshaw! Quinton will never get too far from Tyson or you for that matter," she said, diverting her attention to the shelf of green plants in Angela's kitchen. "He loved Cole like a brother," she said, attending to a plant by removing its dead leaves. "He's such a handsome man, a good-hearted fellow. It's a shame he can't find a decent woman to settle down with."

"I think Quinton has met someone," Angela informed Miss Viveca.

Glancing up at her with interest, Miss Viveca said, "Who? I haven't been in touch with him, but I should make a point of calling him. Shame on me for not keeping in touch! But like I told you, so many things after Cole's death were too painful for me to deal with. Seeing Quinton only reminded me of my loss. I know he grieved him too, but I had nothing to give or offer him by way of emotional support. I had been barely holding on myself." She clucked her tongue. "Now tell me. Who is this that Quinton is seeing?"

"I met her at the wedding. You know, Calvin's wedding. Her name is Taylor Brown. She is a singer and quite popular with the kids. She's gorgeous and..."

"How old is this person?" Miss Viveca asked .

"She's young. I believe she's twenty-one or twenty-two. Something like that."

Miss Viveca sighed with impatience. "She doesn't sound right for Quinton. He needs a woman who can offer him more than celebrity, glamour. He needs someone like you. A woman with a good head on her shoulders and the knowledge of what it takes to please a man."

"No, I'm not Quinton's type," Angela snapped.

Placing the plant back on the shelf, Miss Viveca gave her a puzzled look. "I was just using you as a hypothetical example, dear."

Angela laughed nervously. "Certainly."

"Quinton wasn't always the catch he is now," Miss Viveca reflected. "I remember when he signed that big pro contract. He got caught up in the swirl of media attention, the glamorous women, the good life, so to speak. And my Cole was right at his side despite the fact that he had you and little Tyson. No telling what those two got into once they were away from Riley. I can imagine that there were all sorts of temptations for them. Though you and Cole used to act as though things were okay, I could sense that his trips with Quinton caused tension. I knew I wouldn't have liked for my husband to go off for days without me with his single friend."

"You're right. I hated it. I came to resent Quinton. It was easy to blame the problems with my marriage on him," Angela said. "Enough about the past. Let's join Aunt Nadine and Tyson. Oops! I forgot that French vanilla cream that Aunt Nadine loves. Let me get it out of the fridge."

Miss Viveca was near Angela when she turned around from the refrigerator.

Not expecting her to be there, Angela jumped.

"I didn't mean to frighten you. But you should figure out a way to have Tyson spend more time with Quinton."

187

Placing the cream on the tray, Angela lifted it. "Well, Quinton knows how to find us. I'm not going to impose on him," she said in a polite tone of finality. "Let's join the others." She pushed through the door that led into the family room.

Tyson and Aunt Nadine were watching one of those entertainment news programs.

The attractive female announcer said, "Wedding bells for singing sensation Taylor Brown. Stay tuned for the details." The program went to a commercial break.

Hearing this Angela felt a twinge of jealously that she knew she had no right to feel.

Aunt Nadine sat forward in her chair to reach for her dessert Her brown face was bright with curiosity. "Tyson was just telling me that our Quinton has been seeing this pretty girl that these people are reporting on. You think he's going to marry her? They flashed her picture and to me, she looks to be too young for him. That child is a wisp of a thing who looks as though she is barely out of high school." She glanced at Angela for information.

Angela took a seat on the arm of Aunt Nadine's chair. "She's of age, Aunt Nadine. You know how men like Quinton like these fancy women." She chuckled to hide her anxiety about what she feared was about to be announced.

"Shh...the program is coming back from commercial," said Miss Viveca, focusing on the television screen. "I want to hear this."

Taylor appeared on the camera. Looking gorgeous in a white gown, she was being interviewed before performing at a ritzy charity event.

The female reporter held the mike in front of Taylor. "I understand you have a lot to be grateful for today."

Taylor tossed her long hair and blushed. Then she smiled wryly and spoke into the mike. "Oh yes I do," she gushed. She held up her well-manicured left hand to show off her expensive- looking diamond ring.

"Wow! Congratulations," said the reporter. "You must tell us who the lucky man is. Is he that tall, debonair ex-basketball player who's been at your side recently?" the reporter asked.

Taylor hesitated and smiled demurely. "No comment. I must be going. I'll be performing next. I have to get my makeup and hair touched up. Bye-bye," she said, floating away and leaving the reporter.

The reporter looked into the camera. "You heard it here first. Taylor Brown, the latest top selling pop diva will soon be a married lady. Back to you, Melanie."

Tyson turned to his mother and looked relieved. "It's Quinton. I bet it's him." He looked as happy as Taylor.

"Well, isn't that something," Miss Viveca said. "That little flashy girl will never be happy living in Riley. And Quinton is a hometown boy who loves being near his family." She took her dessert plate from the tray and settled back in her chair. "Looks as though there is going to be another wedding in that family. From the looks of

189

that young lady, I'll bet she'll want one of those extravagant fairy tale weddings far from here."

Angela didn't say anything. Her heart was in a swirl of emotions. She admitted to herself that she wanted Quinton and could have had him if she hadn't been afraid of upsetting her son. But Tyson was her responsibility. She had done the right thing, even if she had hurt herself in doing so. Tyson appeared to be less tense after hearing Taylor's engagement announcement. Angela assumed that he no longer feared the threat of having to share her with Quinton. He giggled and laughed with his grandmother and great aunt at some silly comedy show they had turned to. Angela picked at the pie and then set it aside. She pretended to be interested in the program, but her thoughts were elsewhere. She reminisced about the night she and Quinton had made love. She thought of how he had made all the stress of her ordinary life melt away for that one night. She thought of how desirable she had felt and how Quinton had electrified her with his tender and skillful lovemaking. In that one night she had lost her heart to him. She had traded what little peace she had for the misery of loving a man who could never be hers. Her throat tightened with emotion and her eyes burned from the tears that she knew she mustn't shed. She had been so foolish to dare to dream that she could have another chance at love and happiness. That night had been nothing but a wonderful dream that she had to awaken from.

After Tyson's grandmother and aunt left, Angela sat alone in the kitchen drinking a cup of tea and thinking of the news she had heard on the program about Taylor.

Tyson came into the kitchen wearing his pajamas and stared at his mother sheepishly.

She smiled, watching him go to the refrigerator for a cool drink before he went to bed. The two hadn't done much talking in the last few days. And she had been grateful that while Tyson was still cool toward her he hadn't acted obnoxiously in front of the relatives.

Once Tyson had poured himself a glass of juice, he leaned against the refrigerator door, eyeing his mother.

Angela sensed he had something to say. "Is there anything you'd like to say?"

Tyson finished off his drink and set the glass aside. He went to the table and stood near his mother. "When I peeked in the kitchen to see what was taking so long with the dessert, I overheard you and Grandma talking about Dad and you. I listened for awhile." He placed his hands on the back of the kitchen chair. "You and Dad...you and Dad weren't as happy as I thought, huh?"

As casually as she could manage, she said, "Your father and I both loved you dearly. But there were problems between us, son. Before he passed, we both realized that we no longer made each other happy. And we had plans of getting a divorce."

Tyson winced and lowered his eyes. He dropped down into the chair and folded his arms and buried his face. He began to sob.

The sound of his tears broke Angela's heart. She leaned toward him and draped her arm around his shoulder. She encouraged him to look at her. When he did, she took a napkin and wiped his tears. "I know the truth hurts, son. But it was the way it was. I'm sorry you had to overhear this instead me being straightforward with you sooner. I know how much your father meant to you. I wanted you to never think any less of him for the problems he and I had. He was a good father and you know he loved you. That's something you'll have always. It's special and no one can ever take that from you. I know you're too young to understand the adult problems, but one day you will. I want you to find comfort in the fact that both your father and I loved you with all of our hearts. Okay?" She gave him a warm smile to reflect the immense love she had for him.

Tyson rose from his chair and threw his arms around her neck. "I'm sorry for everything, Mom. I...I love you," he said in a barely audible tone.

With tears streaming down her face, Angela tightly embraced her son. "Oh Tyson, I love you too, son." In that moment, Angela knew that she and her son could move forward and resolve the problems that had threatened their relationship.

Chapter 11

The Friday after Thanksgiving, Angela's spirits were lifted not only by the reconciliation between herself and her son, but also by the fact that so many people had chosen All of Our Best to shop for Christmas gifts. From the time the store opened at ten that morning until she put up the closed sign at seven o'clock, there had been a constant stream of customers. The store was a wreck and she and Christina had given up trying to replace books on shelves. They just went to the open boxes in the storeroom to get whatever they needed. Angela had to take orders for those books from the Blackboard Bestsellers' List that she had run out of in the afternoon. She sat on the stool behind the counter feeling exhausted yet ecstatic, sipping on a cup of tepid coffee. "Christina, we're going to have to get some help for the holidays. There's no way you and I can handle things if they are going to be as busy as today. I am so pleased that our community has taken a liking to the store."

Christina slipped out of her shoes and leaned on the counter. "You've got all the great Black books right here. You know what people and especially the female customers want to read. And they like the idea that you have read just about everything you have. You can make recommendations for them that makes their shopping more enjoyable and easier."

"Well, I love books. That's why I chose this business," Angela said. "Let's leave this mess until the morning. I want you to come in an hour earlier. That way we can have some time to straighten things up. Do you have a responsible friend or relative who'd want to work for the season?" Angela asked. "We need some help badly."

Christina nodded in agreement. "I can ask my cousin who is home for the holidays. She'd love to make some extra money."

"Good. Tell her to come on," Angela said. "Go on and head home. I'll bet you want to catch up with that boyfriend of yours."

"Well, we are going to the movies. If I leave now, I'll have time to get a nice hot shower and freshen up before the nine o'clock show in the mall." She rushed to the back and got her coat and purse. Standing near Angela to slip on her coat, she eyed her boss. "Will you be all right by yourself? I can stay until you're ready to leave."

"No, go on. I'll be fine. I'm going to get these special orders ready to call in first thing in the morning. There's no need for me to rush home. Tyson is spending the night with his grandmother and great aunt. They're taking him shopping, so that he can show them all of the expensive things I won't buy him and that he hopes they'll surprise him with." Her weary face broke into a smile.

Christina giggled. "That Tyson is something else. I see him around and he's becoming quite a hit with the girls his age. The girls are all crazy about him. He's a player in the making."

"Please don't tell me that. I sure hope he won't grow up to be one of those guys who wants to play with women's emotions." She moaned at the thought and shook her head. "Go on, Christina. Have fun on your date." Angela followed Christina as she headed for the door, so that she could lock it behind her.

Just as Angela unlocked the door for Christina, Quinton appeared and slipped into the store past Christina.

"Hey, Mr. Que," Christina said. "How have you been? Haven't seen you in a while."

Quinton made his way in and stood near Angela. "I'm fine, Christina. Just fine. Going to meet your guy, I bet."

"Yeah, I am. We've got plans." She grinned. She

stared at Angela who wore a dismayed look from the unexpected appearance of Quinton. "I've got to go. I'm glad you're here to keep Angela company. Now she won't have to be alone while she works."

"See you in the morning, Christina," Angela said, urging her employee with the mischievous look in her eyes out the door.

"Good night," Christina said as Angela closed the door and locked it so no more customers would think she was open. She stood at the door until she saw Christina get safely in her car. All the while, she could feel Quinton watching her. She wondered what had bought him to the store when he should have been at his own business where there were probably plenty of customers for him to deal with on such a commercial night as this. And then again, shouldn't he be off with Taylor? Hadn't he mentioned something about attending one of her concerts for the weekend? she thought. And what about the two of them celebrating that engagement that Taylor had revealed on that entertainment show Thanksgiving Day? she wondered as she watched Christina pull away. She heaved a sigh to calm herself to face Quinton. Her heart had stood still the moment she had seen him stroll into the store. Turning away from the door, she met his gaze.

"What brings you here? I would think you'd have too much to do and too many important people to see to come to my humble store." She walked away from him and headed for the counter where she wouldn't have to be near him. She was afraid that he would hear her heart pounding or see the longing in her eyes for him.

Just as she went past him, he snagged her wrist. "I had to come see you. I wanted to know how Thanksgiving was for you and Tyson." He smiled with beautiful candor.

She didn't want to be affected by his smile or his wonderful eyes, but he had set her pulse to racing. "It was nice. Really nice." She eased her wrist away from his touch. "Miss Viveca and Aunt Nadine came for dinner. And for the first time in years, she was civil to me. She gave me a chance to feel close to her." She hurried to go behind the counter. She had to put some distance in between them. "And best of all, Tyson and I talked about his father and have begun to resolve things that have been keeping us at odds. Yes, I have more than enough to be thankful for."

"That's great! I'm happy for you." Quinton followed her to the counter and he gave her a puzzled look. "Why are you acting so strange? You're treating me as though I might harm you or something." He stared at her intently.

Angela glanced at him and saw concern written all over his handsome face. Any other time she would have welcomed his interest, but she didn't want him to care. She didn't want anything from him now that she knew he belonged to another woman. She turned on the radio. A sweet and classic soul ballad filled the store and cut the silence and the tension she felt.

All of a sudden, Quinton was behind the counter. He took hold of her arm and touched her face to encourage her to look into his wonderful, kind eyes. "Stop running from me and from what you know you feel," he said in a firm tone.

She frowned and recoiled from him, wishing she could hate him. But she felt herself drowning in the tender emotions she was struggling to resist. "Why won't you leave me alone? You have someone. You are engaged. I refuse to be...I can't be used."

Quinton looked baffled. He rubbed the back of his neck. "Where did you get this engagement business from? And what makes you think I would dare to use you, Angela?"

Angela's face was flushed from her mixed emotions. She breathed deeply. "The news was on television. Last night Taylor was on that entertainment program. She showed her engagement ring and..."

He gave her an incredulous grin. "Tell me, did you hear her say that she was engaged to me?"

"No, I didn't. But you have been seeing her. She sang at your father's wedding and..."

He stepped closer to her. His hands were locked behind his back and he stared at her with a glint of amusement. "For your information, Taylor is engaged. But I wasn't the one who gave her that rock she is sporting. You see, she is engaged to a baseball player whom she dated before she and I dated casually. His name is Mason Harrison. He plays for the Atlanta Braves."

Her mind whirled from his revelation. "You and she aren't..."

Quinton shrugged. "See what happens when you jump to conclusions? A lot of people thought that I was the guy she alluded to on that program. I've gotten calls from my friends across the country. Even Tyson called me this morning and asked me..."

Hearing her son's name, she held up a hand and a smile tilted the corner of her sensual mouth. "You got me, Quinton. I guess you got a kick out of seeing me make a complete fool of myself."

He strolled up to her and gave her a look full of tenderness. He brushed her face with the back of his hand. "You're cautious, but no one's fool."

Angela was mesmerized by the way he stared at her and the gentleness of his touch. She felt a tingling in the pit of her stomach and her heart swelled from the tender emotions she had been repressing thinking he had an interest in Taylor. "I can't bear to be hurt any more." She peered into his comforting eyes.

Taking her hands in his, he lifted one to his lips and kissed her fingertips. "Oh my sweetness, the last thing I want to do is to hurt you." He enfolded her in his arms and held her close to his heart. His arms were strong and comforting about her. Angela could no longer restrain her need to return his embrace. Hugging him, she looked up at him with tears sparkling in her lovely eyes. "Do we stand a chance? My world is far from perfect. And what about Tyson?"

He cupped her chin and smiled. "Whose world is perfect? Tyson is a growing boy. I'm sure he'll adapt. I don't want to be his father. Of course, I'll be there to guide him and help him to become the kind of man that you and Cole would be proud of." He looked deep into her eyes, conveying his sincerity. "I love you, Angela. I want you to understand that. I want to accept all the responsibilities of what it is to love a wonderful, beautiful woman like you. I want to pamper you and protect you. I want to be your everything because you are someone who has held a precious place in my heart way before you even became aware of me."

Angela was overwhelmed by what she heard. She had never known the kind of love that Quinton was offering her.

Holding on to her, he kissed the corner of her mouth. "Are you willing to give me a chance and to allow me to share your life? Tyson and I have already talked and he was cool with the idea."

She had closed her eyes to relish the sound of his voice and the feel of his kiss. Her eyes flew open when she heard that he had spoken to Tyson about them. She reared back slightly. "You've talked to Tyson. He didn't say a word to me about that. I spoke to him earlier today too."

"I sort of made him promise not say anything. It was a man-to-man thing." Quinton placed his hands on the sides of her neck. "So, it's all up to you now."

"It looks as though I don't stand a chance against either of you." She chuckled. Then she grew somber. She reached up and held his face. "I'm willing to give it a chance. You sneaked into my heart and I can't stop thinking about you." She breathed deeply. "I've fallen in love with you. I didn't want to. I was afraid to, but I love you," she admitted. Her declaration lighted her eyes.

Quinton's face glowed with happiness. "Phew! I thought you'd never say it." He locked his arms around her waist and swung her around, laughing with gusto.

Angela felt deliciously alive from the joy she saw on Quinton's face. He set her on the floor and swept her against him. He fitted his mouth over hers and gave her a lingering kiss that sang through her veins. She responded with an urgency that satisfied her soul and spirit.

Quinton took a breath, fixing his eyes on hers. "I don't just want to be your man, I want to be your husband," he said in a sensual tone. "I can't imagine my life without your precious love." He peered into her eyes with anxious anticipation.

Angela was overcome and she fell upon his chest. Tears of joy spilled from the corners of her eyes. She was so happy that it frightened her, yet thrilled her to the core. She felt the caress of his hand on her hair and she beheld him affectionately. "Oh Quinton, I'm yours. I

201

want to be your precious love forever and always," she said in a sweet voice full of tenderness.

Nothing was left to be said. Quinton reclaimed her lips and he crushed her to him, sending spirals of ecstasy through her with the passion of his kisses.

Angela's heart leapt with joy from the whirlwind romance that had changed her life. She relished the excitement of it all. It was a marvelous feeling to be loved, she thought, clinging to him. At last, she would know real love and have a marriage that she was sure would be heaven sent.

-end-

INDIGO

Winter, Spring & Summer 2001

January

Ambrosia	T. T. Henderson	$8.95

February

The Reluctant Captive	Joyce Jackson	$8.95
Rendezvous with Fate	Jeanne Sumerix	$8.95
Indigo After Dark Vol. I	Angelique/Nia Dixon	$10.95
In Between the Night	Angelique	
Midnight Erotic Fantasies	Nia Dixon	

March

Eve's Prescription	Edwina Martin-Arnold	$8.95
Intimate Intentions	Angie Daniels	$8.95

April

Sweet Tomorrows	Kimberly White	$8.95
Past Promises	Jahmel West	$8.95
Indigo After Dark Vol. II	Dolores Bundy/Cole Riley	$10.95
The Forbidden Art of Desire	Cole Riley	
Erotic Short Stories	Dolores Bundy	

May

Your Precious Love	*Sinclair LeBeau*	*$8.95*
After the Vows	*Leslie Esdaile*	*$10.95*
(Summer Anthology)	*T. T. Henderson*	
	Jacquelin Thomas	

 June

Subtle Secrets	*Wanda Y. Thomas*	*$8.95*
Indigo After Dark Vol. III	*Montana Blue/Coco Morena*	*$10.95*
Impulse	*Montana Blue*	
Erotic Short Stories	*Coco Morena*	

OTHER GENESIS TITLES

A Dangerous Love	J.M. Jefferies	$8.95
Again My Love	Kayla Perrin	$10.95
A Lighter Shade of Brown	Vicki Andrews	$8.95
All I Ask	Barbara Keaton	$8.95
A Love to Cherish (Hardcover)	Beverly Clark	$15.95
A Love to Cherish (Paperback)	Beverly Clark	$8.95
And Then Came You	Dorothy Love	$8.95
Best of Friends	Natalie Dunbar	$8.95
Bound by Love	Beverly Clark	$8.95
Breeze	Robin Hampton	$10.95
Cajun Heat	Charlene Berry	$8.95
Careless Whispers	Rochelle Alers	$8.95
Caught in a Trap	Andree Michele	$8.95
Chances	Pamela Leigh Star	$8.95
Cypress Whisperings	Phyllis Hamilton	$8.95
Dark Embrace	Crystal Wilson Harris	$8.95
Dark Storm Rising	Chinelu Moore	$10.95
Everlastin' Love	Gay G. Gunn	*$10.95*
Forever Love	Wanda Y. Thomas	$8.95
Gentle Yearning	Rochelle Alers	$10.95
Glory of Love	Sinclair LeBeau	$10.95
Indiscretions	Donna Hill	$8.95
Interlude	Donna Hill	$8.95
Kiss or Keep	Debra Phillips	$8.95
Love Always	Mildred E. Kelly	$10.95
Love Unveiled	Gloria Green	$10.95
Love's Deception	Charlene Berry	$10.95
Mae's Promise	Melody Walcott	$8.95
Midnight Clear	Leslie Esdaile	
(Anthology)	Gwynne Forster	
	Carmen Green	
	Monica Jackson	$10.95
Midnight Magic	*Gwynne Forster*	*$8.95*
Midnight Peril	Vicki Andrews	$10.95
Naked Soul (Hardcover)	Gwynee Forster	$15.95
Naked Soul (Paperback)	Gwynne Forster	$8.95
No Regrets (Hardcover)	Mildred E. Riley	$15.95
No Regrets (Paperback)	Mildred E. Riley	$8.95
Nowhere to Run	Gay G. Gunn	$10.95

Passion	T.T. Henderson	$10.95
Path of Fire	T.T. Henderson	$8.95
Picture Perfect	Reon Carter	$8.95
Pride & Joi (Hardcover)	Gay G. Gunn	$15.95
Pride & Joi (Paperback)	Gay G. Gunn	$8.95
Quiet Storm	Donna Hill	$10.95
Reckless Surrender	Rochelle Alers	*$8.95*
Rooms of the Heart	Donna Hill	$8.95
Shades of Desire	Monica White	$8.95
Sin	Crystal Rhodes	$8.95
So Amazing	Sinclair LeBeau	$8.95
Somebody's Someone	Sinclair LeBeau	$8.95
Soul to Soul	Donna Hill	$8.95
The Price of Love	Beverly Clark	$8.95
The Missing Link	Charlyne Dickerson	$8.95
Truly Inseparable (Hardcover)	Wanda Y. Thomas	$15.95
Truly Inseparable (Paperback)	Wanda Y. Thomas	$8.95
Unconditional Love	Alicia Wiggins	$8.95
Whispers in the Night	Dorothy Love	$8.95
Whispers in the Sand	LaFlorya Gauthier	$10.95
Yesterday is Gone	Beverly Clark	*$10.95*

All books are sold in paperback form, unless otherwise noted.

You may order on-line at www.genesis-press.com, by phone at 1-888-463-4461, or mail the order-form in the back of this book.

Shipping Charges:

$4.00 for 1 or 2 books
$5.00 for 3 or 4 books, etc.

Mississippi residents add 7% sales tax.